THE OPPOSITE OF HERE

Also by Tara Altebrando

The Leaving

The Possible

THE OPPOSITE OF HERE

TARA ALTEBRANDO

BLOOMSBURY
NEW YORK LONDON OXFORD NEW DELHI SYDNEY

BLOOMSBURY YA
Bloomsbury Publishing Inc., part of Bloomsbury Publishing Plc
1385 Broadway, New York, NY 10018

BLOOMSBURY and the Diana logo are trademarks of Bloomsbury Publishing Plc

First published in the United States of America in June 2018 by Bloomsbury YA

Library of Congress Cataloging-in-Publication Data
Names: Altebrando, Tara, author.
Title: The opposite of here / by Tara Altebrando.
Description: New York : Bloomsbury, 2018.
Summary: On a seventeenth-birthday cruise with her parents and three friends just months after her boyfriend died, Natalie is surprised to connect with a fellow passenger, who then mysteriously disappears.
Identifiers: LCCN 2017043770 (print) • LCCN 2017057845 (e-book)
ISBN 978-1-68119-706-7 (hardcover) • ISBN 978-1-68119-707-4 (e-book)
Subjects: | CYAC: Cruise ships—Fiction. | Birthdays—Fiction. | Grief—Fiction. |
Best friends—Fiction. | Friendship—Fiction. | Dating (Social customs)—Fiction. |
Mystery and detective stories.
Classification: LCC PZ7.A46332 Opp 2018 (print) | LCC PZ7.A46332 (e-book) | DDC [Fic]—dc23
LC record available at https://lccn.loc.gov/2017043770

ISBN 978-1-68119-937-5 (Aus)

Book design by Kimi Weart
Typeset by Westchester Publishing Services
Printed and bound in the U.S.A. by Berryville Graphics Inc., Berryville, Virginia
2 4 6 8 10 9 7 5 3 1

For my Dad, who hates boats

A glimpse into the world proves that horror is nothing other than reality.
—*Alfred Hitchcock*

Hell, to me, is a cruise ship.
—*Benjamin Percy,* Thrill Me

THE OPPOSITE OF HERE

Fade in on me.

I'm in my attic bedroom, and someone's calling my name.

Gaining volume, coming closer.

"Natalie!" All singsong.

"Oh, Nat-a-lie!" Like a horror-movie taunt.

I should have a carving knife tucked under my mattress.

Or a trophy I can swing through the air—a blunt object!—to ward off my attacker.

But I'm not prepared.

My door isn't locked; it's not even entirely closed.

It squeaks at a painful, wretched pitch as it swings open into the room, and I brace myself, clutching a pillow to my chest.

"Hi, Mom," I say.

"Hi, yourself," she says, and she tosses an envelope at me. It lands with a light thud on my bed. I sit up to look.

"It's really happening!" she says, then wanders out of the room muttering to herself, "I think I saw your flip-flops in the garage. And you need some WD-40 for that door."

I lie back down.

I close my eyes.

I said it was too soon, that I wasn't ready to have fun with a capital *F*. But the accident was a solid nine months ago now, and everyone has decided that I need to move on.

I promised I'd try.

I'm not sure I meant it.

I open the envelope anyway.

Congratulations on booking your . . .

✯IMPORTANT INFORMATION✯

PASSPORTS

Travel documentation requirements can vary greatly based on which Starlite cruise you have selected to enjoy, and also on your country of citizenship.

We recommend traveling with proof of citizenship (US or other) and an additional photo ID.

All documents must be valid for the duration of the cruise.

PACKING TIPS

Bathing suit and cover-up, T-shirts, shorts, pants, sundresses, sandals and sneakers, a light jacket or sweater, plus dinner attire. Also don't forget other items you may need: camera, binoculars, sunscreen, hat, etc.

In general, the dining dress code for the week is "Cruise Casual." No swimwear or tank tops (men).

Visit our website to check whether your itinerary includes a formal or semiformal night.

WHAT NOT TO PACK

Firearms or ammunition of any kind. Please do not bring homemade, precooked, or other perishable food items, irons, sporting equipment, balloons, candles, musical instruments, or illegal drugs.

A WORD ABOUT HAND-SANITIZING STATIONS

Cruise ships are particularly prone to rapid-spreading viral infections. Please comply with Starlite's request that all passengers use sanitizing stations frequently, in addition to handwashing.

ALL GUESTS MUST BE ABOARD BY 3:45 P.M. OR YOU WILL NOT BE ABLE TO SAIL.

To disembark at any port, passengers under the age of eighteen must be accompanied by an adult traveler (eighteen or older). If that traveler is not a parent, the Minor Release Form must be on file.

The ship horn moans like a dying animal. The Miami sun is set to broil.

We're all wearing T-shirts my mother had made that say Natalie's 17th Birthday Sail-a-bration, which Paul, like me, would have taken issue with on account of that made-up word, those hyphens. But he's not here. Our "party" includes me, my parents, and my three best friends: Lexi, Nora, and Charlotte, in that order.

The engine has sprung to life, and we're officially unmoored. Everyone around me seems giddy; except perhaps my mother, who is watching me nervously. She wants to see if I'm going to follow through on my promise to at least try.

We are at the "Sail-Away Bash" on the Aquarius Deck, having already dumped our backpacks in our staterooms and completed the ship's mandatory "Muster Drill," where all the passengers gathered in assigned areas to learn about life jackets and lifeboats and where to go and how to behave should the ship start to sink, though nobody actually used the word "sink." We had to walk down six flights of loud white metal steps behind a Staff Only door to get to our assigned "B station," which ended up being the balcony of the ship's main theater.

As latecomers straggled in, I filled the empty stage with actors performing some tragic play. I imagined water starting to fill the theater, lifting their costumed bodies up to us, some of them still clutching props like bouquets and swords and muttering their lines while treading water or grasping at the blue velvet curtains.

Finally, the people running the drill called us to attention. One of them had to tell Nora to put her phone away.

Twice.

Then one more time.

He told us to go ahead and cover our ears while they set off the series of loud beeps—one long followed by six short—that would signal us to return to this station in the event of emergency. I wanted to shout out, *You mean if we're sinking*! But didn't.

Then a different guy, the cruise director, Jimmy, appeared on stage and made an announcement that the drill was complete and the place to be—*the only place to be*—was the Aquarius Deck where the Sail-Away bash was.

So here we are.

I spot the source of the music: three men in lime-green shirts—two playing steel drums, another on keyboard. I think I can almost make out the tune of "Limbo Rock," but I'm not sure; the notes percolate into one another and blend.

Young couples hold babies in tight sun hats with chin straps. Older couples dressed alike in soft clothes stand by the rails, waving at the shore. A big African American family—like twenty people, all dressed in white—poses for a photo. By the bar, some college types and twenty-somethings in groups are licking salt off their hands and throwing back tequila shots. My mother's champagne flute glistens, and a plastic sword stabs fruit in my father's glass; they clink drinks, kiss with fish lips, and say, "Cheers!"

That boy over there is about our age and looks a little bit like Paul at first but then not at all, and my hand goes to my neck, to my favorite necklace. It's a small silver bar with the map coordinates of my favorite beach—the beach where Paul and I first kissed—etched into it. I dropped hints about how much I loved the necklace when Paul and I had passed the shop one time, and I was sure he'd buy it for me for Valentine's Day, but then, well . . .

I bought it for myself in the end and then lied—even a little to myself—and told everyone it had been from him.

~~~

I guess I'd been mad at him, while he'd been off dying without my knowing it. Mad because we had plans to watch the original *King Kong—and* the newer one—that afternoon and he didn't show up and didn't text that he was going to be late or had to cancel. It wasn't like him at all. And we weren't that kind of couple—the kind that fights for dumb reasons, then makes up and does it all over again, not like Lexi and Jason. So after the fact I was mad at myself for being mad.

I should have been *worried.*

I should have been praying or calling hospitals.

I should have been doing anything but just sitting there stewing and texting Lexi stuff like *WTF could he be?*

Where he'd *been* was dead in the driver's seat at the front of a line of traffic that stretched for miles—the kind of traffic that makes people turn off their engines and stand up on their car door ledges, craning their necks to spot whatever small apocalypse must have occurred farther up the road. My father had come home and complained about it all—he'd had to reverse off the highway!—before any of us knew that Paul had caused it when he'd driven into the divider and died on impact.

I still wondered sometimes whether maybe he *had* been trying to text me.

Whether he'd reached for his phone and—

~~~

"Supernova," Charlotte says. "Let's go!"

"Huh-wha?" Lexi says, as if she's just woken up.

"It's the teen lounge or whatever," Charlotte says.

"Do we have to go *now*?" I'm standing by a railing, watching the port of Miami shape-shift. High towers are shrinking. Mansions with bright blue pools are morphing into extravagant dollhouses. I spot a ladybug clinging to the railing for dear life and lift it with a finger, then blow it gently toward shore, toward survival.

You will not die here today, ladybug. Not on my watch.

"Yes, *now*." Charlotte hooks my arm. "There's a meet-and-greet kind of thing. Let's see who shows. I mean, there have to be some cute guys on this ship, right?"

"No one worth hanging out with is going to turn up at a 'teen lounge' called 'Supernova,' " Lexi says, making air quotes twice.

"That may or may not be true," Charlotte says. "But we're going anyway." She turns to my mom and says, "We're going to check out the teen lounge."

My mother says, "Sounds perfect," and smiles happily in my direction.

Charlotte's my mom's favorite because Charlotte's pretty much a mom herself. She's the sensible, cautious one. The least threatening to my mother's sense of what kind of young woman I should be. She wears her hair in a tight low ponytail—every day without exception—and wears high-necked clothes that de-emphasize her chest. She's half-black, and when she first moved to our overwhelmingly white town she genuinely seemed to baffle some kids in school by not looking like her white mom. ("Are you adopted?")

Then she got a little pushback from a tight-knit group of black kids at school for becoming friends with me and Lexi and Nora in addition to being friends with them. She told me once that she sometimes feels caught between two worlds at school—like she has to decide who she is instead of just being who she is—and that she didn't feel that way where she'd lived before, in Philadelphia. She mostly keeps her head down, studies hard, plays by the rules. So when I'm with Charlotte, whose parents are pretty strict, my mom sees at least a little bit of innocence and a lot of caution. When I'm next to low-cut, loud Lexi, by contrast, she sees terrifying things: boys, parties, sex, lies. She's not entirely wrong to think this way. Lexi likes boys and they like her.

Nora steers a middle course, I guess.

Like me.

I smile back at my poor, long-suffering mother because I know this whole thing has been hard on my parents, too. My mother had loved Paul like she would a son-in-law; and she had to watch me go through all of it: the crying—sometimes sobbing until I threw up—the appetite loss, the numbness, the anxiety of wondering what the next bad thing to happen to me was going to be, the slow march back to something resembling normal.

"Stay together, girls," she says. "And have fun!"

~~~

We follow Charlotte, who has a map on some schedule-type thing we apparently get daily. We go up one set of stairs, then in through automatic sliding doors to a carpeted foyer, then into an elevator, where there's piped-in music—Sinatra singing "Beyond the Sea."

Then we're out in a long hall with huge portholes; small children
~~~

are climbing onto their ledges to pose for photos their parents are taking.

We hang a left at a sign for Supernova and go into a darkened tunnel—Day-Glo stars painted in black-light oranges and greens—and come out at a sign-in desk. There are clusters of cushy armchairs and a dance floor lit from underneath by flashing neon lights. There's a disco ball, a fountain soda machine, and a bar area with high diner stools. An adjoining room is an arcade—with huge video game screens on the walls—and a set of glass doors open up to an outdoor area where there's bocce and Ping-Pong.

A perky cruise woman greets us on the dance floor—"Hey, ladies. Where are we from?"—and I drift away to get a drink.

We're the only ones there, so the music is too loud, the air too cold.

But by the time I've found a cup and ice and Coke and a lid and straw, a group of guys have come in and the cruise person starts making everyone introduce themselves, which is reason enough to stay where I am. Two girls who look like sisters come in holding hands and then run around, exploring like giddy children. Then a few kids walk in alone, each looking more confused than the one before them about the poor life choices that they must have made to arrive at this moment. Or maybe I'm projecting. The cruise lady ropes them in, too.

I feel a presence and turn toward it.

He's tall; his chest where my eyes are—and I'm no shrimp at a solid five nine—and he's wide, like he could fold around me the way Paul could. Like a letter and an envelope. He's standing at the soda machine, looking confused. He says, "Harrumph!"

"You need help?" I ask.

Without looking at me, he says, "I'm not seeing the vodka."

A laugh starts to form inside me, but then it falls off a cliff somewhere and lands in a dark valley full of laugh bones. Enjoying myself hasn't been easy lately.

He turns to me and tilts his head and, all chipper, says, "And where are we from?"

Another laugh runs at the cliff, and this one makes it, leaping into the world as a giggle. The sound is foreign, like surely someone else made it.

"*We*," I say, "are from Florida. Near Orlando."

He is studying my breasts; no, my shirt. Or both. "And are *we* Natalie?"

"We are."

His gaze is so direct and unapologetic that it seems rude. It's like he's staring. But it's also true that I'm staring back. I can't remember the last time I met someone new.

He's not just cute; it's something else. There's this confidence to him, like he's an old movie star reincarnated, and everything around him—from the plastic cups to the soda machine to the straws and lids I'd fumbled with—seems to be trying to please him by being fluid, easy in his hands, like maybe the force is strong in this one. He has one dimple—of course—and wavy brown hair and icy blue eyes that look transplanted from a husky. The simple fact of him standing there seems to have awakened parts of me that I thought were long dead.

Hello there, rapid heartbeat.

Nice to see you, tingling skin.

We meet again, sweaty palms.

"*Sail-a-bration*," he says, slowly.

"My mother's idea," I say.

"I wear a medium." His eyebrows curl into a questioning position that I'd only thought possible in animated movies.

Then the song changes and it's a ridiculous girl-power pop anthem and he says, "This is my *jam*. Come on." He puts down his cup and takes my hand and starts to drag me toward the center of the dance floor.

"Wait," I say, laughing but also panicking. "I don't want to—"

"I'm joking," he says, stopping abruptly and turning, and our bodies nearly collide. "So how long do I have to talk to you?"

"Excuse me?" I bristle.

He says, "How long do I have to make small talk before *we* can get out of here?"

"For real?" Wait. He wants to leave with me?

"What's your favorite color?" he asks.

I pick "purple" whether or not it's true.

"Favorite band or singer." He tilts his head and waits.

"Elvis Moriello." A no-brainer.

"Never heard of him," he says. "Favorite movie?"

"*Rear Window*."

"Hitchcock, eh?" He nods approval. "You're too perfect. Favorite book?"

"Too many to name," I say. Too perfect for what?

"Was that enough chitchat?" He smiles. "You *know* you don't really want to be here."

I look around the room; lights under the dance floor mimic fireworks. "You're right. I don't."

But that's nothing new. I have a long history of not wanting to be where I am. Soccer games. School dances. Keg parties. It is possible that that is my dominant personality trait and has been since I was a kid.

There's me throwing a tantrum by the curly slide, not wanting to be at the playground.

There's me being sent to the principal's office, for passing a note in class that read: I AM SO BORED.

There I am, at my grandparents' house for a sleepover, unwilling to unpack my bag.

I once ruined a forgotten friend's birthday party by refusing to help color a sea-life mural *or* play Pin the Fin on Nemo, choosing instead to stand cross-armed by the door under a sign pointing toward "Sydney Bay." And when I was ten, I made such a stink about not wanting to go to the mall one day that my parents followed through on their threat of going without me. After getting over the initial shock of being left alone, I didn't much mind it.

The only place I actually wanted to be in recent history was wherever Paul was, and that isn't an option anymore.

He'd have hated this cruise.

I hate this cruise.

He'd have walked right past a teen lounge, and I would have followed.

Now, I imagine him up in some cloud-throne in heaven, looking down on the ship—a tiny blip of white on the vast ocean; and me, even tinier. He's laughing and shaking his head like some bemused saint.

"Oh, Natalie," he's saying. "What have you gotten yourself into?"

What indeed.

"Just give me a number," the boy in Supernova says. "Five minutes? Ten?"

~~~

After I finished packing yesterday, I went over to Lexi's house to help her do the same, because if she'd been left to do it on her own we'd likely all have missed the boat.

We put her open suitcase on the bed and systematically started to fill it. We were sailing from hot to hotter and back—Miami, Grand Turk, Nassau, a private Starlite Cruise Line island, Key West, and back—so it was all sandals, tank tops, shorts, sundresses, bathing suits, and cover-ups, plus a cardigan or hoodie or two for over-air-conditioned dining rooms or chilly nights. When she'd opened her underwear drawer and pulled out multiple sets of coordinating lacy thongs and bras, I did a double take.

"Um," I said.

"What happens on cruise ships stays on cruise ships," she said.

"Wait. What do you mean?"

We first met back in kindergarten and went to school together for a few years, but then Lexi moved and I sort of forgot about her until she moved back and started high school with us. I saw her on the first day of freshman year, and she ran up to me and threw her arms around my neck and then pulled away and did a quick Irish jig, and it felt like she hadn't changed at all, which was ridiculous because something like six years had passed, but she still had this kid-like goofiness about her that made it sort of funny when she was talking about things like thongs. She's good at getting herself in dumb situations—forgotten wallet, lost textbook—and being
~~~

bewildered by it all, like she's somehow been cast in the wrong movie.

"I *mean*," she said, "if I meet someone. Well. I just . . . I don't want to break up with Jason, not exactly, so, you know. I'm allowed a little fun if the opportunity comes along, right?"

"I guess," I said, feeling bad about feeling judgy, especially because the reality was that she and Jason were not a great couple. She seems to physically shrink around him, while he puffs up; it's like there's some set amount of space they can take up and it's out of balance pretty much all the time.

"Don't go getting all judgy on me," she said.

"I'm not," I said.

She gave me that look of hers, the one she gets to make when she knows I'm lying.

"You'd really cheat?" I still didn't like the idea of it.

"I'm open to the possibility is all." She drew her hair up into a ponytail, then adjusted her breasts in her bra. "You should be open, too."

"To what?" I held up one of her thongs. "This?"

"Exactly!" She snatched it from me. "Come on." She went to leave the room.

"Where are we going?" I asked.

"Victoria's Secret," she said. "Because whatever you have going on under there"—she pointed in the general area, swirled her hand around—"it's probably got cobwebs in it."

I crossed my legs, then uncrossed them. "That's a horrible thing to say."

"I know," she said. "But I'm *so tired* of walking on eggshells about it all." She made a funny face and tiptoed exaggeratedly around the room.

"Fine." Anger lit my face, then immediately started to recede. I was getting tired of it, too. Of being alone. Of feeling dead and dusty. Of no one at school even daring to flirt with me or like me because dead boyfriends are hard acts to follow.

"Fine," she said.

We finished packing, then went shopping. And when I got home, I threw out every pair of underwear, every bra that Paul had ever glimpsed or touched. I packed up a week's worth of new secrets.

~~~

"I just met you." My feet are dark silhouettes on the dance floor. "Why would I want to go anywhere with you?"

He holds my gaze blankly, like he is a robot reading data about me with his eyes. I use all my powers to transmit a blank *poker face poker face poker face*. Then he picks up his cup, takes a long sip from a straw, and puts it down. "Suit yourself."

He starts to walk toward the exit.

"Wait. Where are you going?" I grab his arm.

His robot gaze analyzes my touch.

I let go.

"I don't know yet." He looks around the room. The perky cruise person is whipping and nae nae-ing. Possibly, wait for it, yes: dabbing. My friends are watching her, laughing into their hands.

He says, "What's the opposite of here?" and looks like he's expecting an answer.
~~~

Over on the dance floor the counselor is—no, please. Just *stop* . . . Gangnam style?—and when I turn back, he's gone.

~~~

"And here's the birthday girl now!" Lexi says when I join my friends and the guys they've met, then she starts to make introductions.

"This is Nate," she says. "He is under the false impression that he can beat me at whatever video games they have in this place." There's this sparkle in her eyes that she gets when she's flirting, but at least she keeps her shape, doesn't cave in on herself the way she does around Jason.

Nate smiles and says, "Nice to meet you."

Then Lexi says, "That's Leo. And that's—"

Brett? Bennett? A new, louder song has started.

We all sort of nod and half wave, and Lexi keeps talking to them—mostly Nate—and it sounds like they're all around our age and are here with their parents who are old friends, like used to be college roommates. There are younger siblings they plan to avoid elsewhere on the ship.

Leo seems to be focused on Charlotte, who is not really allowed to date—so good luck to *you*, sir!—but then Nora flips her hair and smiles at him. Which could be a big *uh-oh*. Then again, Nora hasn't liked anybody in forever so it probably won't be an issue.

"Where have you been?" Lexi turns to me as the others all go back to whatever they were talking about before I walked over.

"I was over there," I say. "Talking to a guy."

"Ooh, which one?" She casts a glance around the room.

"He left," I say.

"Was he cute?" she asks.
~~~

"Very," I say, still feeling tingly from his . . . newness. Or maybe just from laughing after so long. "And funny, too."

"Well, where is he?" She turns so she's standing beside me, sharing my view.

"I told you, he just left."

"Why?"

"You really have to ask?" I say and I dab. "He wanted me to go with him, but I wasn't sure."

"You big dope." She elbows me. "Go! Live a little. We'll be right here."

"But go where?"

"It's a ship, Natalie." She shoos me away like I'm a child. "And he just left. He can't have gone very far."

~~~

We're all aboard Starlite Cruise Line's *Pisces*, a ship that holds thirty-five hundred passengers and twelve hundred crew.

In the frantic few days before we left, Charlotte, who fights anxiety about new experiences by being hyperprepared, insisted we look at every photo on the website and watch video tours of the boat. That's how we know that there are: Waterslides. Shuffleboard courts. Movie theaters. Shops. A bar made entirely of ice where they give you fur coats to wear. Four different dining rooms. A small planetarium.

We know that onboard activities include everything from cooking classes to painting parties to improv shows and trivia nights. There are seminars on how to fold towels into animal shapes, ballroom dancing demos, and karaoke and trivia contests. There are fireworks one night—my birthday! Woohoo!—and even one of
~~~

those "escape room" experiences: a murder mystery you have to solve in an hour.

The main entertainment area, the Starlite Boardwalk, is on the uppermost deck and mimics an old-timey pier—it has a carousel and ice cream and candy shops and funnel cake stands and games like Skee-Ball and pinball and the balloon race with water guns.

One level down from there toward the back of the ship is the Aquarius Deck, where a tube ride hovers above the pools like a massive clear serpent. I will not be going on it. Ever since Paul died, I've been experiencing a sort of vertigo or dizziness whenever I'm in motion, mostly when riding in the passenger seat of a car.

I'd suggested at the outset of the planning "something fun" for my birthday that maybe a cruise wasn't the best idea, all things considered, but my mom said most of the time you don't even feel like you're moving. So she'd started keeping an eye on rates and dates around my birthday, and I put the girls "on call." We were basically waiting for the deep discount you can get if you book last-minute as Florida residents to go deep enough for my parents, which it finally did.

"At this point it's practically cheaper than staying home," my father had said, and that had decided it. I called the girls and told them it was "go time" in three days, and my mother went out and bought boatloads of Dramamine and seasickness bracelets for all.

~~~

Back through the Supernova tunnel, I'm dumped on a hall heading toward the pools again, so I go with it. It leads me back to the Sail-Away bash, where the steel drums have been replaced by a DJ
~~~

blasting a wordless dance track—electronic drums spitting out a beat.

The two main pools are packed with people, laughing and splashing; a toddler wearing a Nemo bathing suit in a kiddie sprinkler area wipes out and starts wailing and is rescued by his mother's lean arms.

I go down a winding staircase when I seem to hit a dead end, scanning the crowd as I go.

He's not there.

I pass through a set of automatic sliding doors into the level below Aquarius and walk through a crowded corridor of slot machines, their dinging loud and annoying, like a pack of battery-operated morkies.

In a piano lounge, a small but committed crowd surrounds a man playing a shiny black baby grand; they are waving their drinks and belting out that song about a piano man—seemingly without irony.

I end up at an elevator bank and spot a map. I stand there trying to locate myself.

"Excuse me?"

It's a girl who looks maybe nine or ten, holding a gold and black card of some kind. "I need to stand there."

"Ellie, don't be rude," her mother says. Then to me, "Sorry."

I move and the girl steps purposely onto a golden disk on the carpet. She holds her card up, and a painting on the wall reveals itself to be digital; it gives her a clue about a mystery involving a bag of stolen stars while her parents wait with smiles. When they move on, I step back to the map and locate Supernova. Using my finger I find what looks like the opposite of it.

The Gemini Deck at the rear of the ship on the third level.

I get into yet another elevator and go down, and the feeling of it all transforms my stomach into a surging sea of excitement. The car stops and an old couple goes to get on, then backs off.

"Sorry," the woman says. "We have no idea where we're actually going."

I nod and smile.

Ditto.

~~~

I go out through a set of heavy glass doors and step out onto the Gemini Deck, but there is no one there—everyone's too busy having fun in more exciting spots. My lungs cave with disappointment. I thought I'd figured it out. I thought for sure this was where he'd be.

I take a few deep misty breaths. We're actually really moving now. Like if I were to jump, I'd land in a different spot. I'm too afraid to actually try it.

I walk toward the back of the boat and watch the ship's impossibly massive white wake—like a Jacuzzi for a giant.

Florida has been reduced to a melted blob on the horizon, and the sun has dialed it down to roast.

Maybe I should take a lesson from it and calm down some.

I feel dumb.

I'll see him again another time.

Or maybe I won't.

It's just a cruise. Just a week. Just a guy.

So dumb.

I should go get the girls, go back to the cabin, and get ready for dinner.
~~~

I turn.

"I thought you'd be at least a few minutes longer, you know, like in an attempt to seem all cool and aloof."

He is lying on a lounge chair that I wasn't able to see when I came out, tucked to the side behind a thick winding staircase to an upper deck.

"Sorry to disappoint," I say.

He nods at the chair next to him and reaches out to pull it closer to his. "Park 'er here."

I walk over, sit down, and stretch out my legs. My skirt is too short; I pull at its edge but it's no use. I just can't move . . . much.

"So, Natalie, tell me. Is this *sail-a-bration* of yours what you always dreamed you'd do when you turned seventeen?"

"Definitely not, no," I say.

"Well, then, why are you here? What went wrong?"

I consider lying, but something in his eyes makes me not want to. I say, "My boyfriend died."

He looks pale and stricken for a second and we lock eyes for too long and then he looks away, shakes his head. "I am not often rendered speechless."

"Sorry," I say.

"Did you kill him?" he asks, turning back to me.

"What?" I snort involuntarily. "No. Of course not."

"Then what are you sorry for?"

I spot a cloud that is barely holding it together as a cloud. "For telling you that like within the first few minutes of even knowing you. I just mean, I don't want to be a downer. Sorry."

"Yeah, seriously." He turns and sits sideways on his chair, *so very close* to me. "That was an *awful* thing to do to me. To make up for that *egregious* oversharing you just did, you're going to have to spend the next"—he looks at his watch—"half hour with me."

"Oh, I am, am I?"

He stands. "I am expected to dine with my parents at six, and I can hardly show up in such a fragile state."

"Well, all right, then." I stand and he doesn't move, so we are face-to-face, or face-to-chest, and I'm feeling too much *something*, so I look away and squeeze out from between the chairs.

I mutter, "Excuse me."

I've completely forgotten—or maybe never knew—how these things are even supposed to work.

~~~

I met Paul on a class trip to the Clearwater Marine Aquarium. There were enough kids in our school that you didn't really know everyone in your grade. I'd seen him around and thought he looked normal—tall with bad posture to try to make it less obvious how tall—and he usually seemed happy, which was more than most of us could say.

Winter—the dolphin with the prosthetic fin made famous in the *Dolphin Tale* movies—was the aquarium's big draw, but I found him—or maybe he found me—by the tank of a freakish-looking moray eel, its mouth permanently agape.

"It looks like it just told a joke and is waiting to see if you're going to laugh," he said, and I smiled.

"I'm Paul," he said, without hesitation.

"I'm Natalie," I said, in the same matter-of-fact tone.

"You know what's always bugged me about this place?" he said.
~~~

"What?" I was surprised but not unpleased with his frankness.

"Clearwater *Marine* Aquarium," he said. "Like what other kind of aquarium would it be? Like for real. Is that not to be confused with the Clearwater *Alien* Aquarium? What?"

I shook my head, quite seriously. "No, it's because of the Clearwater *Human* Aquarium down the road. You haven't been there?"

"Would you believe I haven't?"

"Then we'll have to go sometime," I said. "You really have to see the newborn baby tank. It's the cutest."

"Oh my god," he said, laughing.

"What?" I said.

"There is such a thing as going one step too far," he said. "And *you*? You took that step."

I shrugged.

He said, "But you'll still take me there, right?"

"Sure," I said, and then we both nodded and it felt like something bigger and real had been decided.

We rejoined our classmates then, and Paul met the girls after Nora pinched me and asked, "Who's *that*?" and we met some of his friends and then we all visited with Winter and learned about the science behind the fin that saved her life and Paul and I exchanged numbers and within the space of a week we went to a movie together and went to the beach together and kissed. We were boyfriend and girlfriend just like that.

~~~

"So this is the part where I say something like 'What was he like?' or 'How did he die?' Right?"

"I guess so," I say.
~~~

We've found shuffleboard courts. He is pulling equipment from a rack. He hands me a long pole with a curved plastic head on it.

"So, um, what was he like?" he says.

"You know what?" I say. "I don't want to talk about him."

"Okay, then." He puts a disk at my feet. "You know how to play?"

"Nope."

He sighs exaggeratedly, shakes his head, and puts his hands on his hips. "Do I have to do all the work in this relationship?"

I laugh; it feels easy now. "Are you always like this?"

"You mean, am I always *this amazing*?"

I roll my eyes.

He explains the rules and we each take a couple of turns and I'm not a complete disaster but the mood has changed and I'm not sure why.

"So what are *you* doing here?" I ask, brightly, trying to change the mood back. "On a cruise, I mean?" I smile. "You have a T-shirt?"

"No T-shirt, alas." He slides his disk and it lands on a ten. "I have business to attend to in Key West."

"Oh, you do, do you?"

"Is that so hard to believe?" He's faking hurt.

"In fact, it is." I take my next shot; the disk slides onto the ten, knocking his out of play.

"Well, you don't have to believe it," he says, readying his next disk. "Makes no difference to me."

"You already said you're with your parents. So—"

"So maybe it's family business," he says, and his disk flies and lands on a fifteen and I think it means he's won. Then we play another game, not really talking except for stuff like "nice shot" or "no fair!"

After I win—I think?—he looks at his watch. "I need to go," he says, putting his pole back in the rack and starting to collect the disks.

"Yeah, me, too," I say. I also have dinner at six.

He turns to me, and stands close. "But for the record, I am not."

"Not what?" I ask.

"Always like this," he says.

I nod, waiting to see what he'll say next. For a moment he's just looking at me; if I don't consciously inhale and exhale I might stop breathing altogether.

"What about you?" he says. "Are you always like *this*?"

Words bubble up from a secret place inside me. "I don't even *know* what I'm like."

"Well, this week you can be any way you want to be, right?" he says.

"Well . . . my friends are here."

"Ditch those bitches!" He holds up a hand for a high five.

I smile and comply. "Done!"

"There you go!" he says, with fanfare, then we're quiet for a minute as we go inside and he seems to be studying me for updated data and I have a harder time finding my poker face. "It sucks, I know. Being this person who ends up being defined by some kind of tragedy."

"Yes." My throat clogs. "Yes, it does."

"Where's your cabin?" he asks.

I tell him my stateroom number.

"Not even close," he says as he hits the elevator up button.

I hit down.

"What do you miss most about him?" he asks as we wait.

"I said I didn't want to talk about him." My necklace itches and I adjust it.

He says, "I think you're lying."

"Maybe," I say.

"It's his giant penis, right? He had a giant penis?"

"Oh my god, no. Just stop." I push him and he stumbles backward laughing. I am laughing, too—echoing clear across that canyon inside me.

I like this feeling. I like being surprised by someone.

Surprised, too, by myself.

"Okay, so he had a small penis," he says. We are both still laughing. "A very small, very soft penis. But surely he had some redeeming qualities?"

"He did," I say, wiping away tears of laughter. "For one thing, he always knew how to make me laugh."

"Small penises will do that."

We both lose it again then finally stop. My stomach hurts, like it just did crunches.

"This is fun," he says as his elevator arrives.

"Yes, it is," I say.

"Rematch later?" he says.

"Wait," I say. "Who even won that last game?"

"Doesn't matter," he says. "Nine o'clock?"

The doors close before I can say, "Yes," but I say it anyway.

The boat lurches; I grab a railing, then step into my elevator feeling like maybe cruises aren't so bad after all.

It's time to unpack and settle in for the ride.

★ THE STARLITE STARGAZER ★

Welcome aboard the Pisces!

Mandatory GUEST ASSEMBLY Drill; report to the station indicated on your key card at 4:00 p.m. You will not need to wear a life jacket, however you must bring your STARLIGHT KEY CARD. All ship services are suspended between 3:45 and 4:30.
ALL GUESTS MUST ATTEND

Today's highlights:

4:30 p.m. — Sail-Away Bash on the Aquarius Deck; LIVE MUSIC!
5:00 p.m. — Meet and Greet in the Supernova Teen Lounge
5:00 p.m. — KIDS' CLUB OPEN HOUSE AND TOUR featuring Dance Floor Fun and Ice Breakers

Walking Ship Tours leave the Atrium every hour on the hour starting at 5:00 p.m.!

7:00 p.m. — '80s Music "Name That Tune" in the Lunar Lounge
7:30 p.m. — Movie Theme Song "Name that Movie" in the Supernova Teen Lounge
9:00 p.m. — Celebrity impersonator Chris Montell in the Starlite Theater

Shops open when we reach international waters!

I wave my key card in front of the lock and it clicks open. Charlotte is in the shower; Nora's out on the balcony; Lexi is wearing two towels—one as a turban and one wrapped around her torso and tucked near an armpit. She is reorganizing stuff in her suitcase. "Well . . . ?"

"Found him."

"And?"

"And I don't know." I flop down on the cabin's only bed. "He's pretty great. Like maybe amazing. I seriously don't think I've felt this way about anybody since—"

"Whoa, Nelly!" Lexi looks up as she flips her suitcase lid closed.

My hot skin reacts to the air-conditioned cabin with a chill. "What's *that* supposed to mean?"

"You just met the guy. So, like, hold your horses."

"Of course I just met him. We just got here."

"Okay so don't get all ga-ga over the first guy you meet is all I'm saying." She starts to slip clothes on, releasing her towel.

I look away. "I thought you wanted me to move on," I say. "Out with the cobwebs and all. You're the one who told me to go after him!"

"Yes, because we're here to have fun in the sun," she says. "We are here to *let loose* and flirt with whoever. We are *not* here to get all lovey-dovey and serious."

"I'm not," I say, weakly.

The four of us are able to share a stateroom because Charlotte, who had different school-year cutoffs in Philly, is actually a year older than us and just turned eighteen. So technically we're within the ship's regulations. Our parents also filled out the minor release forms so that we can disembark without them as long as Charlotte's there. (It also means she can buy alcohol on board, but my parents didn't seem to note that detail the way we did.)

Lexi and I will be sharing the bed while Nora and Charlotte sleep in bunks—one is the converted sofa; the other pops down from the ceiling to reveal painted constellations.

The staterooms on our hall are serviced by a man from India named Bonny, who introduced himself while double-checking that all our bags had arrived. "I'm here or near here all the time," he said. "Anything you need, I'm your guy."

The room is maybe half the size of my bedroom at home but has a balcony, at least, which will help with the sardine feelings and claustrophobia I anticipate. You can even see a part of the captain's bridge—basically a glass chamber—that juts out a bit farther than the balconies do.

There's more closet room than we have clothes to hang—and a small safe that we don't use—but not a lot of drawers; we each get one so will mostly live out of suitcases. It took us a few minutes to figure out that the lights only work if a key card is in this holster by the door. There are two tiny bathrooms—one with a toilet and sink, the other with a shower and sink—and one framed illustration on the wall. In it, a group of people on a tropical island are looking out to sea, waving to a departing cruise ship.

Lexi, now dressed, says, "Oh, and your parents were looking for you in a panic. So you should probably pop your head in over there and tell them you're alive. Maybe tell them to try to chillax a little, too?"

"Yikes." I lean up on an elbow and study the *Stargazer* schedule on the bed. "Where did you say I was?"

"Shopping."

"It says right here that shops don't open until we're in international waters after dinner."

"Well, I tried," she said, shrugging and flopping her arms at her sides.

I stand to find clothes for dinner *and* for my rematch. "I wish you could be a little more excited for me."

I'm trying to sound more reasonable than I feel. I pull a dark purple sundress out of my suitcase.

"You're right. I'm sorry." She bends to release the towel on her head and shakes out her hair. "I can't wait to meet him."

I'm an idiot.

I don't even know his name.

~~~

When I told our film teacher, Mr. Cassidy, that the four of us were going on a cruise for my birthday and would be missing school, he asked me, "Have you ever seen *Lifeboat*?"

"No," I said. "What is it?"

"Hitchcock film shot entirely on a boat," he said. "Not my favorite Hitchcock except they're all my favorites, as you well know. Oh, and there's an episode of his TV show set on a cruise ship, too. You should check them out."

It's true that we'd studied nothing but Hitchcock for the first few weeks of class, or at least it felt that way. But I hadn't minded. I'd gone in as a fan, having seen *The Birds* and *Vertigo* on a classic movies channel; class only helped me to better understand why I liked them.
~~~

"What about *The Poseidon Adventure*?" Mr. Cassidy said. "Not Hitchcock, mind you, but relevant."

"Nope," I said. "What's that?"

"Shelley Winters? Oscar-nominated role?"

"Not ringing a bell," I said. "Sorry."

"Sometimes I don't know why I bother with you kids today."

"Why? What's the big deal?"

"Look it up," he said. "The original one. Not the remake."

So I googled it and found out that it was a movie from the seventies set on a cruise ship. A rogue wave hits the ship and it's overturned and it starts to sink—upside down. A small group of survivors inside the boat set out for the ship's hull—hoping for a miraculous rescue at the surface of the sea.

I found it on YouTube and watched it, up until a point where an obese woman character—the Shelley Winters role—has to swim through a flooded corridor in order to attempt a dangerous rescue of another passenger and she has a heart attack right after. It was painful—I cried—and I was too pissed off at Mr. Cassidy to finish watching and I told him so in class the following week.

"You can't just give up on a movie during the dark night of the soul," he'd said.

"What's that?" I asked.

"That's the point in a film when all hope is lost and the protagonists must dig deeper than ever before to prevail against the odds stacked against them."

"Too late," I said. "Gave up."

"Trust me," he said, "you'll go back to it. You'll want to know what happens. You'll need to know."

~~~

I put my dress on, then go out into the hall to knock on my parents' door since we all decided it was best not to use the adjoining door in case someone was *in flagrante delicto* (my father's phrase) or "otherwise indisposed" (him again).

"There you are," my mother says. "We were worried."

"Mom," I say. "Where would I go, exactly? And I'm turning *seventeen*. I need at least a little bit of free rein."

"I know, I know." She nods. "I'm sorry. I just want this week to be special."

"It already is." It's the right thing to say.

The girls pour out into the hall, and I feel for a second like the ship surged or dipped. We four spend an awful lot of time together at home. We have almost all our classes together and three of us are in driver's ed together and a different three are all on yearbook and glee club and then we still choose to hang out on weekends. When my parents suggested the cruise, it was obvious to me and to them that if I brought anyone I'd have to bring three. It was true that things with Nora had become a bit strained in the past year, but no one seemed to notice that but me. Not even Nora, frankly. But none of the four of us has ever spent a whole week together, so this is uncharted territory. No way to know whether it'll be smooth sailing or choppy seas.

My parents walk ahead and my friends surround me.

"I thought you said you weren't ready to meet anyone," Nora says, so I guess Lexi told her what I said.

I nod. It was true that I'd been saying that for a while. "Maybe I was wrong," I say.

"Did you make, like, plans?" Lexi asks.
~~~

"We said we'd meet up later, yeah." Like it's no big deal.

"We're doing movie-theme-song trivia," Charlotte says. "You should come. You'll know more than us anyway."

"I want to be on Nate's team," Lexi says.

I smile. "Are you calling dibs?"

Lexi winks. "Maybe."

I say, "Maybe you should 'whoa, Nelly' yourself."

"It's not like that," Lexi says.

Nora looks at me and says, "Oh, like you've never called dibs."

I seriously have no idea what she's talking about. "What are you talking about?"

"Never mind," she says, but I don't brush it off so easily.

She was there when I met Paul.

But I didn't think I'd had to call dibs.

~~~

Crew members greet us by the dining hall with containers of sanitizing hand wipes. This is a thing we read about in our travel documents—a policy implemented after a whole ship got knocked out by a norovirus. As much as I hate the fake lemon smell of the wipes—and believe, like my parents, in good old soap and hot water—I'm happy to cooperate if it means we avoid spending the whole week taking turns hugging the john.

Our official dinner seating every night is at six, which means if we want to see shows we see the late show. We will rotate through four different dining halls, designated by letter codes on our key cards; our head server and assistant server circulate with us. We can skip the official sit-down meal and opt for some more casual buffet and to-go foods if we want. There is one optional formal
~~~

night—which happens to coincide with my actual birthday—so we all brought one fancy dress.

Tonight we've been assigned the Stargazers' Garden. It's massive, like it easily holds five or six hundred people. There are small tables for two with candles glowing in red glass, big round tables for larger parties like ours, and other configurations in between. There are mirrored walls and columns, reflecting lights and silverware and smiling faces, and a gazebo at the end of a sort of garden path lined with gorgeous floral arrangements and small trees. The ceiling is impossibly high-feeling considering we're on a ship; it's dark blue with tiny recessed lights that twinkle like stars; piano and chatter and the *whish* of a fountain fill the air.

We take seats and our waiter introduces himself—Carlos, from Belize—and I wonder if he thinks of this as the opposite of Belize. At the next table a man with a thick Southern accent is saying that the room was inspired by the gardens of Versailles at night, but he pronounces it "versails" and I cringe. Then I order prime rib—*"For the Landlubber!"* the menu suggests—and wonder if Carlos is also cringing. How is landlubber even still a word?

A ship photographer arrives at our table and snaps pictures of my parents—"and now the girls." We smile once, then again. We say "cheese" when told to.

My parents have brought a list of all the land excursions, so we review the activities we've already booked. Tomorrow is a designated "fun day at sea," but the day after that we'll go snorkeling in Grand Turk, then the next day we visit a waterpark resort—The Reef—in Nassau; then there's a day on the private island, another day at sea, and we'll cap it all off with a stop in Key West, where we'll take a tour of Hemingway's house.

"There may also be a surprise or two thrown in along the way," my mother says conspiratorially to my father.

Great.

I scan the room again.

I don't see him and there's no reason I should, I guess. I didn't even think to ask his name, let alone his dining room assignment.

During dessert at least four birthdays get celebrated around the room, with staff members clapping and singing.

"I don't want any of that," I say as I watch an elderly woman snuff out a candle. I wonder if she made a wish or not. "No singing. Understood?"

My parents both nod, but they don't look happy about it. After dessert, they excuse themselves to go play a game of '80s Name That Tune in a bar somewhere. "You girls will be okay?" my mom asks.

"Of course," we all say, like a Greek chorus.

My father says, "Back in the cabin by midnight."

The chorus nods.

"So," Lexi says when they're gone. "Is he here?"

"I don't see him," I say.

"Well, we'll meet him soon enough," Charlotte says.

"I don't know about the theme song thing," I say.

"*What* don't you know?" Lexi asks.

"I just mean, I'll ask him. But I don't get the sense that it'll be his vibe or something."

"What's his vibe?" That's Lexi again. "Anti-movies?"

"I don't know," I say. "Just more low key."

"You barely know the guy, Nat," Charlotte says.

"I know!" I also know all too well that I should be wary of guys I don't know very well, but this feels different.

"We need to meet him," Lexi says.

"We absolutely need to meet him," Charlotte says. "Just go get him when it's time and bring him to the lounge."

"Okay," I say. "I will."

I look at one of the room's large columns, and wonder if it would be sturdy enough to climb if I had to escape rising waters like the folks on the *Poseidon*.

~~~

We head for the shops, which have just opened up; there's a festive feeling about it all, like it's Christmas Eve and everyone is on a frenzied hunt for last-minute stocking stuffers.

We pop into a clothing store to look at hoodies for Nora, who forgot to bring one, but she doesn't see any she likes. We look at gowns in the window of a dress shop; even the mannequins seem embarrassed at the level of tack: so many sequins. We pass a candy shop and a tie shop and a jewelry store and a flower shop and then Lexi decides that it's time to test out Charlotte's alcohol-purchasing abilities.

We go back to the cabin and pull out the room service menu, and Charlotte gets on the phone and orders a "bucket of beers."

"I'm not sure this is a good idea," I say. We sometimes have a beer or two at parties, so it's not that. It just seems more like there are rules here. Like this is on par with going to a bar, which we'd never think to try at home.

"It goes onto my key card charges," Charlotte says. "My parents are so busy all the time, they won't even look at the bill—if they even get an itemized one. I'll just make sure I buy some souvenirs and stuff."
~~~

"Anyway, it's only a six-pack—that's like a beer and a half each," Nora says. "What's the big deal?"

"Fine," I say. "I thought Charlotte would be the one saying no."

"I'm always saying no," she says. "I want this week to be different."

I guess that makes two of us.

When there's a knock at the door, three of us hide in the bathrooms and Charlotte answers.

Then, giggly, we head out to the balcony and the water is lit up like a tropical pink drink and life feels like this wild and unpredictable sort of thing.

I think I like it.

~~~

Our punishment, as Mr. Cassidy called it, for missing four days of school in the middle of November is this: each of us has to shoot a two-line film while on board the ship.

Exactly two lines of dialogue.

We each have to turn in a properly formatted script—likely a page or less—and show the film on our return.

"How are we supposed to do that?" Charlotte said when we were given the assignment.

Mr. Cassidy wagged his phone in the air. "Surely at least a few of you have iPhones? With cameras?" He knew we all did.

He went on a tirade against the "Falling in Love montage" that day, complaining that it's a cop-out to just show two people doing a bunch of cute things together while some happy/dramatic song plays and expect audiences to believe they're falling in love. He said it was a screenwriter's responsibility to put the chemistry on the page.
~~~

We talked about tropes that day, too. And he suggested that we could each find inspiration, potentially, if we identified some of our favorites. Along with the rest of the class, we put together this master list of tropes on the smart board.

Man against nature. Dark family secrets. Limited settings. Big comic misunderstandings (misheard dialogue). Stories about "chosen ones." Star-crossed lovers. Class wars. Holy Grail–type quests. It went on and on, and when we were done we were each asked to pick our favorite storytelling trope.

"Technology run amok," Lexi said. "Always a good time."

Mr. Cassidy smiled.

When it was Charlotte's turn she went for "underdogs."

Nora picked "star-crossed lovers."

Finally, Mr. Cassidy turned to me. The words on the board seemed to swim. I said, "How do you pick just one?"

~~~

He isn't at the shuffleboard courts at 9:01 or :02, and for a second I am ill with nerves—or am I mildly seasick? Or wait, buzzed?

I stand by the edge of the ship, then back away.

I'm allowed to have a little fun. Like Lexi.

And he *will* show.

I have no reason to believe he won't, even at 9:06.

I imagine Paul on his cloud-throne again, and wonder what he'd think of all of this—of me waiting on a guy. Of me, moving on. A tide of anger rises in me because I'm angry that I even have to move on. For once I had actually liked where I was.

I take my phone out of my small purse—phone, lip gloss, key
~~~

card—because I want to take a picture. I say, "You'd do the same thing."

"What, exactly, would I do?"

I almost drop my phone in the Atlantic.

Not a reply from the heavens, no.

The relief that he turned up is like a first inhale after an accidentally too-deep dive. He's wearing cement-gray shorts and a short-sleeved white linen button-down shirt. He looks easily three years older than he did earlier and 200 percent more handsome. "I'm sorry," he says. "Were you having a moment?"

"I was," I say. "And you saved me from it."

"Uh-oh, not a good moment, then?"

"Not the best," I say.

Then he says, "I've got chairs over there. I was having a Coke and got you one."

As we move toward the chairs, I say, "For a second I thought you weren't going to show."

"For a second I *wasn't* going to," he says, unbothered.

"Oh no?" I say.

A father and son start to take out the shuffleboard equipment, but whatever. I wasn't that interested in a rematch anyway.

"No." He smiles broadly; his teeth straight like soldiers. "I mean, I was sitting here and looked over and saw that you were here and I was reminded of just how hideously ugly you are. I mean, for real are you like part troll or something?"

"Hey!" I elbow him. It's only funny because I know it's not true. I'm no bombshell—though I *am* super blond with blue eyes—but I'm no troll either.

"But then I felt bad." He turns to face me straight on when we arrive at the chairs. "I mean you looked so lonely. This sad, lonely half-troll girl—"

"Quit it—"

"And, well, I'm a nice guy. So I stuck around. Do trolls even *like* Coke?"

"Well, thanks. Thanks a lot. And yes, yes we do."

"Hey, where are your friends anyway?" He hands me the soda and walks to the railing and I follow. "Shouldn't you all be *sail-a-brating*? I feel bad I stole you away."

"Movie-theme-song trivia. They want to meet you."

"Ah, but do *I* want to meet *them*?"

"Why wouldn't you?" I laugh.

He shrugs. "I don't know. Do *you* want me to meet them?" He drains half of his drink.

"Of course," I say, "and also, not really."

"Aha!" He smiles. "You *do* want me all to yourself."

"Who *are* you?" I say.

He takes a second to think, then says, "Who do you want me to be?"

"I want you to be you."

"But what do you want me to be *for you*?"

"I don't understand," I say.

He shrugs. "I saw you. At dinner."

"Why didn't you say hi?" So he's in the same dining hall rotation after all.

"Didn't feel right. You looked, I don't know. You looked like you were somewhere else and it wasn't a happy place and I wasn't sure I'd be welcome there."

"*Really?*" I think back on our meal, on my mood.

"Don't take this the wrong way but have you, like, talked to someone about it? Like a professional, I mean?"

"I haven't felt the need." A simple truth. "I mean, yeah, I've been sad. And mad. But my parents and friends have been great, so it's okay, all things considered." I can say anything. "It was a car accident. So, you know, I didn't get to say good-bye, and that still feels hard."

"Good-byes are overrated," he says, with a dismissive wave of his hand.

"I don't think so." I shake my head.

"Oh, hey, boyfriend," he says in a high-pitched voice. "I know you're going to die and that this is the last time I'm ever going to speak to you and the next bunch of days and weeks and maybe even years are going to suck big-time but I really just wanted to take a moment to say good-bye because that'll really make me feel better about losing you forever."

"All right, all right." I smile. "I guess I see your point. You ever lose anyone?"

"I lost my dad," he says, and I am about to reach for his arm or hand and say something, but I'm not sure what since the stuff people say is all so dumb. But then he says, "It was only for a couple of hours, though, at the mall. I found him in the food court."

"Come *on*," I moan. "Be serious."

"Here's the thing about loss," he says.

"Enlighten me," I say sarcastically.

He smiles surprise at me. "The ones that really sting are simply the ones that weren't supposed to be next. There's an order to things. Great-grandparents. Grandparents. Great-uncles. Old people first, you know? Men before women; it's only polite. Anyway, I'm just saying there's nothing particularly tragic about a ninety-nine-year-old dying. Unless by some miracle her mother was still alive, you know? We only get upset when things happen out of order. It's all about who's next in line to die for each individual experiencing the loss."

"Next in line to die," I say. "You're serious. This is your theory?"

"Yes and I stand by it."

"Who's next in line for you?"

"One grandparent who's hanging on. Then my parents. Ideally, my father first, then my mother. Then my older brother."

"You're crazy," I say. "And you still didn't answer the question."

"No, I have not answered." He turns to me. "And I would rather not, if that's okay. At least not now, not yet."

"Of course," I say.

He turns to face the water, and we stand silently for a while. He leans over the railing, and I panic and reach for him, grabbing his shirt to pull him back. He's too tall to lean like that. The railing should be higher.

"Easy," he says. "I just want to look straight down."

"Why?" I ask.

"I don't know. The water has a . . . hypnotic, for lack of a better word, allure."

I let go.

He's right that the ocean is officially too big, too deep, too mesmerizing. You can lose your way just looking at it.

He says, "We're something like eight stories high."

"I can't look." Then it's as quiet as it can be with the white noise of waves and wind and the boat's engine.

"I didn't know it would feel like this," he says.

"Didn't know what would feel like what?"

"Being inches from death." He turns to me abruptly, and I almost gasp at our closeness; his gaze so intense, so direct. "What's it like?"

"What's *what* like?" I say, sort of laughing. "You're not making sense."

He looks down at those eight stories again. "Falling in love."

Oh.

"It's hard to explain," I say.

Is it possible it feels like *this* and I've forgotten? Or never knew?

Maybe I never fell, and just was.

He says, "Anyway, dollface—"

"Whoa-whoa-whoa," I say, shaking my head. "You talk to girls like that? For real?"

He shrugs. "My girlfriend doesn't mind."

I'm not going to be able to hide my disappointment; my poker face crumbles.

"But she has an inflated sense of self . . . being an inflatable doll and all."

Relief again. "Oh my god, do you ever stop?"

"As I was saying, *dollface*. It's time for us to take a dip in the pool."

"Excuse me?"

"I honestly don't know how you expect to go in a hot tub wearing that."

"Who said anything about a hot tub?"

"I did." He walks over to a lounge chair. "Just now. Please try to keep up."

I follow and sit, balancing my phone on the vinyl strips of the chair, near my back. I put my glass down on a small side table and he does the same with his.

"Your phone won't work this week," he says. "You realize that."

"I do," I say. "I thought I might want the camera."

"Hashtag cruisin', hashtag blessed, hashtag latergram?"

"Something like that." I try to take his picture, but he pulls his shirt collar up over the front of his face and puts up his hands.

Muffled, he says, "You need to go put on a swimsuit."

"What about you?" I say.

Now he lifts the bottom edge of his shirt to reveal he has swim trunks on under his shorts; the glimpse of his belly skin makes me tingle.

"I am nothing if not prepared," he says. "Now go." He waves his hands at me, shooing me away.

"Okay." I stand. "Be right back. Hey, what's your name anyway?"

He crosses his arms on his chest. "When you come back, I expect you to have three amazing guesses. But here are a few clues. It's not Chico. Or Xavier. Or Angus."

I smile and nod. "Noted."

I'm about to go when he calls out, "Natalie?"

I turn and he stands up and looks really seriously at me for a minute and then he says, "We should say good-bye."

"But I'm going to be right back."

"Just in case."

"In case of what?"

"Rogue wave? Alien abduction? Iceberg? Romaine? Anyway, *you're* the one who's such a big fan of good-byes."

I smile. "Good-bye, dollface."

"Well done," he says, and nods, then he sits back down in his chair. He lifts the leather bar tab holder from the table. "Oh, hey, can you just leave this on the bar on your way past?"

"Sure." I take it from him, slide it on the bar, which doesn't actually appear to be open, as I pass.

~~~

When I step out of the elevator on our stateroom level, familiar voices float to me.

"Just give it time. You'll get over it."

Heavy confusion slows my steps.

"What you do is you box it up and you push it out yer window."

Yes, that's definitely Lexi.

"I'm *trying*."

And that's definitely Nora.

"Box. Window. Done." Lexi sounds firm.

"Okay, okay." Nora is annoyed but resigned.

They round a corner and nearly bump into me.

"Jesus," Nora says.

"Aaaaah, you scared the crap out of me," Lexi says, grabbing my arm with one hand and putting her other hand to her heart.

"What are you guys talking about?" I ask.

"Nothing," Nora snaps, and Lexi doesn't offer up an answer beyond that. She just says, "Seriously, I think I just lost a year of my life."

Maybe they were talking about the awful night I had at Nora's house about a year ago, a night she and I have never actually spoken about. But maybe it's finally time to get it all out in the open? I've told myself that if I give it time, I'll get over it, too. Maybe the same thing happened to her.
~~~

I say, "Where's Charlotte?"

"She's saving our table at the trivia thing. What are you doing back here?"

"Changing into my swimsuit to go hot tubbing."

"Atta girl!" Lexi says. "That's more like it."

"You said you were bringing him to trivia," Nora says.

"Changed my mind," I say.

"Well, have fun and be smart," Lexi says.

"Always," I say, except then realize I left my phone up on the deck chair. So maybe not always. I wasn't smart that night at Nora's house either.

"Come on," Nora says. "We're late."

"Why are you back here anyway?" I ask.

"I needed a sweater," Nora says. "So I borrowed one of yours. Hope that's okay?"

"Of course," I say. "What's mine is yours." She gives me a funny look as she slides my sweater on.

~~~

I head out again after I've put my suit on.

Skipper, Alvin, and Rhys will be my guesses.

Or maybe Hercules, Vernon, and Han, as in Solo.

My phone is right where I left it. But there is no sign of him. I sit down to wait. Maybe he had to go to the bathroom. It would have been nice if he'd thought to bring my phone with him. Someone could have stolen it.

Something white—a towel?—flutters on a chair farther away.

No, not a towel.

I walk over for a closer look, and it turns out it's his shirt.
~~~

I reach for it, and I don't know why but I hold it close to smell it—salty sweat and some woodsy cologne. When I pull it away I see I've left a tiny pink smear of lip gloss on it.

Crap.

I sit with confusion for another minute before it occurs to me that maybe this is a bread crumb trail.

I head off in search of hot tubs, following signs and climbing an outside set of metal stairs to an even higher deck. I find two hot tubs—sending steam up into the air—beside a long bar. There are four people in each tub—lobsters in a pot—but none of them is him.

The bartender is wiping up a thick red liquid.

"Can I help you?" he says as I approach.

"Was there a guy here, like, a few minutes ago? Around my age? Really tall? Possibly not wearing a shirt?" I hold the shirt up to lend my story more credibility.

He shakes his head. "No, sorry."

"Are there any other hot tubs on board?"

"Just the one on the Aquarius Deck, miss. By the tube ride?"

"Okay, thanks."

You can't get there from here, at least not easily. I have to go in and then up four decks, then out again. The tube ride is lit up and otherworldly, like I've stumbled into an alien movie and this is the futuristic science lab.

When I look over at the hot tub, all I see are breasts. They belong to five or six older girls in bikinis, sitting with their feet in the tub, holding drinks. So a different kind of movie.

I wonder what's going to become of me and my friends after high school.

This is pointless.

I go back up to the Gemini Deck for one last look. I put his shirt back where I found it. The moon lights a strip of sea like a searchlight. Cresting white waves bob and fade.

I sit until it'd be too embarrassing to still be here if he did show up.

He's not coming.

~~~

"That was fast," Nora says. "Wait. Why are you dry?"

"He wasn't there." I join them at their table with their boys in the lounge. The movie game answers are being revealed, and people are ticking off their choices as correct or not. A blip of the *Titanic* theme song plays, and it seems to me like a poor choice to have in the mix, all things considered.

"Whatever," Lexi says. "Asshole."

Nora has checked off the *Titanic* answer on her sheet as correct.

"I'm tired," I say, because my anger has subsided and my heart is trying to squeeze between ribs to hide. I'd been foolish to let myself get so worked up. "I'm heading back to the cabin. Anybody want to come?"

"Soon," Nora says as the announcer says, "This was our next clip," and the room fills with high-pitched orchestra sounds that feel ominous.

"That one," he says, "was *Vertigo*."

Nora x's her guess off and says, "Should've known that one, I guess."

"Charlotte?" I ask, thinking she's more likely to want to turn in early. She has a habit, on Fridays, of making plans with us—movies,
~~~

bowling, whatever—then deciding when she gets home from school that she just wants to stay in with her parents.

"Soon," she says to me, and she indicates a table near us with exaggerated eyes, so I look and see two guys. They're black and look like brothers or maybe cousins—something in the cheekbones—and one of them looks Charlotte's way.

"Okay," I say. "Have fun."

She nods and smiles. "I plan on it."

~~~

The engine's rumble lends the bed a cheap-motel Magic Fingers mattress vibe. I lay there, under a heavy comforter, like an X-ray blanket, and hope my irritation gets shaken out of me. I picture my skeleton—in black and bright white—floating around in the middle of the sea like cartoon fish bones.

Below us, I picture weary whale moms pulling their offspring out of our way with gentle warnings—"Now just let it pass, then we'll be on our way."

I see egotistical sharks racing alongside us and winning—*Suckers!*

Somewhere, maybe an octopus who doesn't like his kind marinated and grilled is shaking eight, fisted tentacles up at this ridiculous floating monstrosity.

Or maybe they don't notice us up here, barely skimming the surface of the deep blue sea where they live, not even registering for those still-undiscovered species that live in caves and corners where light never shines.

It'd be better that way.

I close my eyes, and hope that when I wake up I'll be transformed
~~~

into someone who wants to play trivia games and have sing-alongs and *sail-a-brate.*

Someone who wants to *be here* and doesn't care whether she sees him again or doesn't.

When the girls come in, I pretend I'm already asleep but in my head I'm scripting a two-line movie.

~~~

INT. CRUISE SHIP -- CABIN -- NIGHT

A teenager--this is NATALIE--awakes. She looks out the balcony doors, sees the moon is bright. Glances at her friends, still asleep. She gets up, pulls a sundress over her camisole and underwear, slips on flip-flops, and tiptoes to the door, leaves.

INT. CRUISE SHIP -- HALLWAY -- NIGHT

She walks down the empty hall, slips into an open elevator.

EXT. CRUISE SHIP -- DECK -- NIGHT

She spies a teenage boy--let's call him FINN. We sense she's been looking for him. She approaches. He's asleep. She nudges him with her knee. He wakes up.
~~~

NATALIE

You stood me up.

FINN

It'll never happen again.

He sits up, they share a meaningful look. They kiss.

FADE OUT

★ THE STARLITE STARGAZER ★

Pisces Day 2!

We hope you'll enjoy today's FUN DAY AT SEA!!!

Highlights:

7:00 a.m. — Sunrise Yoga with Jan on the Gemini Deck
8:00 a.m. — Pools and tube ride open! Mission to Mars rock climbing wall opens!
9:00 a.m. — Shuffleboard Tournament sign-up on the Aquarius Deck
10:00 a.m. — Footprint analysis in the spa followed by spa services raffle
11:00 a.m. — PORT SHOPPING TALK

Matinee movie: *A Star Is Born*

3:00–5:00 p.m. — Live music in the Atrium: CORAL AND THE REEF
8:00 p.m. — "00Songs"—a cabaret performance like no other in the 360 Degree Theater
9:00 p.m. — Supernova dance party
10:00 p.m. — MARRIED COUPLES' GAME SHOW CHALLENGE—Atrium

Over breakfast in the Saturn Room—basically a floating diner—it becomes impossible to avoid admitting that I don't know his name.

"*I* know his name," Nora says, then she sips cranberry juice.

"What?" I say. "How?"

"It's Richard Furbraines," she says, putting her glass down. "People call him Dick."

The rest of us stare blankly.

"*Dick for brains*?" Nora says, like it's so obvious.

We all crack up; people at the next table stare. My friends and I share sheepish looks, and then Nora says, loudly, "People need to *loosen up*. It's like they don't know they're *on a cruise*."

This is New York Nora. She lives deep inside Florida Nora and takes over her host body a few times a month, usually just to curse in Italian. New York Nora was born on Staten Island and moved to Florida just in time to start high school. She has a New Yawk accent and an Italian-from-Italy grandmother and should totally be on a Mediterranean cruise and not a Caribbean one. She has olive skin—which she of course shares with Florida Nora—and long brown hair with blond underlayers. Her nose is notable and sharply angled, as if carved by a sculptor—but one who had maybe planned for a slightly larger face.

She says, "I think this calls for a round of What's His Deal?"

This is a game we play in film class sometimes, to talk about how to flesh out character motivation and backstory. If we have any extra time at the end of class, Mr. Cassidy will give us a character's name and age—sometimes a profession or situation—and asks us what's his or her deal?

"Yes, yes, perfect," Lexi says, making miniclaps excitedly. "I'll go first."

"Can we just . . . not?" I say—because I want to believe there's a perfectly good excuse; because I have my own fantasies about who he is and don't want anyone else's—but it's too late.

"His name is Stephen and he's from Brooklyn," Lexi says. "He's on the cruise with his parents and his sister who is a sophomore at Harvard. He is like the opposite of her—a total underachiever, smokes a lot of pot—and his parents like her better. Because *of course.* His father is a psychiatrist and his mother is a museum curator. He once did something really awful to some expensive piece of art at an opening, like when he was five or six, peed on a sculpture or something, and his mother has never forgiven him. They sent him away to sleepaway camp every summer of his childhood and are basically counting the days until he goes away to college next fall. They don't even care where he goes as long as he's gone. They're taking a cruise because it's the parents' twenty-fifth wedding anniversary and the parents are hoping their kids will entertain themselves on the ship and pretty much leave them alone. Also, they figured that with the ship's security measures and strict alcohol policies, they won't have to deal with the fact that Stephen has a drinking problem."

"Next!" I say, and I sip my drink. The game's more fun when the person isn't real, isn't someone you maybe like. I'm already ready to be done with it.

"Let her finish," Nora says, then she turns to Lexi. "So what happened last night?"

Lexi is preparing her bagel with annoying precision, spreading butter ridiculously uniformly across the surface. She then takes a bite, chews, and swallows.

"Last night," she says, "he was waiting for Natalie to come back but his sister turned up with a bucket of beers or a bottle of wine or something and she offered him a drink and he couldn't refuse. But he didn't want Natalie to meet his sister or maybe didn't want his sister to meet Natalie so he left and then got drunk."

She wipes her mouth and looks around the room. "He'll probably waltz in here any second now, wearing dark sunglasses and looking pale, and he'll need a greasy breakfast and a beer or two before he'll feel halfway normal again. And when Natalie confronts him about last night, he'll lie and say that his parents found him and dragged him to some dumb comedy show with them. Then he'll act all cool and distant and he'll be cagey about making plans and Natalie will realize he's a jerk and move on. Life's too short—and a cruise is definitely too short—to waste on some loser."

She looks up at me, then; they all do.

I put down my fork—I'm not really hungry anyway—and clap slowly three times. "That was a very nice piece of fiction," I say.

"My turn," Nora says.

"You guys," I moan. "Come on. Let's go *do something*."

"Rock climbing?" Charlotte suggests, looking up from the daily schedule.

"Sure," Lexi says.

"Really?" I say.

"Why not?" Nora asks.

"We never go rock climbing at home. Why here? I was thinking we'd hit the pool? Get a good spot?"

Nora says, "Please don't tell me you're going to want to sit there all day looking for this guy."

"Of course not." I stiffen. "Anyway, you can do whatever you want to."

Lexi stands. "Rock climbing, *then* pool. All of us. Together."

"Fine," Nora says.

"Fine," I say.

~~~

Up on the Boardwalk Deck, we find the Mission to Mars wall, which I guess is supposed to mimic the planet's rocky terrain. Starlite really knows how to work a theme.

We have to get fitted for climbing shoes and harnesses, and it all takes longer than I thought it would. The wall is sort of an indoor/outdoor setup that looks maybe three stories high. We're given a quick lesson in belaying—which means one of us is on the ground controlling the harness as another of us climbs—and how you communicate. You say "On belay" when you're hooked up and then "climbing" to indicate you're on the move and need some slack. When you're done you're supposed to say "lower" or "lowering," which is obvious enough, I think, that it's silly we're being taught it.

Lexi climbs with me on belay. She's a natural athlete—she plays softball and soccer at home—and scales the wall effortlessly. She rings a bell at the top, then bounces down like she does this every day.

When she says she has to find a bathroom I end up climbing with Nora belaying for me.

I don't even really want to but it's like there's this inertia about it
~~~

all because the guy's giving us instructions and everyone else is doing it and I'm here so I may as well?

So I concentrate hard on the climb, on my grip. I learned from watching Lexi that it seems to work better to let the feet do most of the work and have the hands follow. I climb and climb, at one point grabbing a "rock" that looks like an alien face. It startles me at first—someone's idea of a joke—and I hesitate to grab the Martian and almost slip off the wall.

I'm concentrating so hard that I don't actually realize how high I am until I'm within reach of the bell. I look down and my panic triggers vertigo spins.

Someone's shouting, "Go for the bell," but I'm frozen. I can't do it. Can't move a hand. I can't think of the word that I'm supposed to say to the belayer.

"I want to come down," I manage, but the rope remains tight.

I close my eyes and feel the world spin and one of my feet slips and I drift out from the wall and grab my way back.

"I want to come down!" I yell.

Their voices rise and blur.

She says she's done.

What?

Let her down.

She's supposed to say—

Just let her down.

The rope slackens, and I jump down and hit my knee hard on the Martian face. I arrive at the ground feeling angry. I struggle to unhook myself with shaky hands that have tightened up like I've betrayed them by doing this at all.

"What's wrong?" Lexi asks.

"I was trying to get down forever," I say.

"You're supposed to call out 'lower' or 'lowering'!" Nora says. "And anyway, it was only like thirty seconds."

"Can we just get out of here?" I say.

But where's Charlotte?

She's over there. She's climbing hard and fast, with one of the guys she'd had her eye on at trivia belaying for her. When she comes down he says, "Nice climb," and she smiles this free sort of smile I swear I've never seen on her before and says, "Thanks."

She spots us and says, "I've got to go" to him, and then strides over to us.

"Who's the guy?" Nora asks.

"Oh, that's Shaun," Charlotte says, sounding uncharacteristically relaxed. This week is going to be different for her after all.

"Come on," Lexi says. "Let's hit the pool."

"You couldn't tell that I was freaking out?" I say to Nora on the way back to the cabin to change.

"No," she says. "I couldn't."

~~~

We find four loungers facing the main pool and settle in with sunscreen and lemon waters and magazines. Charlotte and Nora go swimming right away, but I'm not hot enough. Or so I say.

I watch and wait, scanning the crowd with secret service–level commitment. *If he's here, sir, I'll find him.*

"You coming in?" Lexi asks me more than once. Then she pokes
~~~

me a few times and says, "Come on. All the cool kids are doing it." But I just say, "No, I'm good."

After a while, they decide to brave the tube ride. I say, "Have fun" and do another sweep of faces.

"You're seriously not coming?" Nora says, standing and taking off her hat.

"I'm seriously not coming," I say. Where the hell is this guy?

"Why not?"

"I don't know. I'm not in the mood."

"But if you never try it, you never know if you'll like it."

"I know that I don't want to. Isn't that enough?"

"I'm not sure it is," Nora says.

"I'm not sure I even know what we're arguing about," I say.

She shakes her head and walks off; Lexi follows after shrugging at me. "You're really not coming?"

"I'm really not coming!" I repeat, then I roll my eyes when she turns to leave.

It's like Sydney Bay all over again; I haven't changed a bit.

I add the tube ride to my scanning area. Maybe he's been zooming around over my head and I didn't know it. I've been sleeping on the job after all.

Now that I'm alone, it officially feels like a stakeout.

Conversations drift by . . .

Oh, no, we still have the house in Pennsylvania.

I heard she was blond. And naked.

I hope she doesn't drop an f-bomb in kids' camp.

But I am focused in my task. I only get distracted once, when two crew members and a captain-looking type with a hard hat on talk urgently to one another, like intrigue is afoot. Hopefully not the dreaded norovirus.

A bearlike middle-aged man with thick, dark body hair sinks into the pool in front of me, then pushes back into a float.

A young mom struggles to put sunscreen on a squirmish girl with white-blond hair, like mine.

A lounging elderly couple with hats and sunglasses are either sound asleep or dead.

It's a solid twenty minutes before Lexi and Charlotte appear in the clear tube overhead. They sit up and look down and wave at me, and I hurry to take their picture, then they disappear behind the ship's massive smokestack.

Nora appears next. She's in a tube on her own, and she doesn't look down at me, doesn't wave, only faces straight ahead. I don't take a picture.

They come back and talk about how fun it was and how I really have to try it, and then Charlotte says, "Can it be my turn? I'm feeling inspired."

"Your turn to what?" I ask.

Lexi puts on a broadcaster voice and says, "To play *What's His Deal?*!!!!"

Charlotte spreads her towel on her chair, sits down, and closes her eyes, then opens them and puts sunglasses on, then lies back again. "He's from California."

I groan.

She keeps going. "His name is something boring beyond belief, like John. He's here with his dad, who's divorced from his mother and is an out-of-work Disney performer–type guy who is probably gay. They've never really bonded, but Mom insists her ex take his son on a vacation every year, and this is it. The dad likes cruises because he doesn't have to pay so much attention to the kid, like if it were just the two of them on some road trip or something. The mom hasn't handled the divorce well at all. She's dating some boring guy who's rich and she lords that over her ex, but he knows she's miserable and so does her son."

Lexi and Nora are listening and chuckling while they wring their wet hair out.

"You've all gone crazy," I say. The captain dude is back, marching with purpose across the deck, jaw clenched.

"Anyway," Charlotte says, "last night, he was up there waiting for you to come back and thinking about your hot body and then he remembered *he has a girlfriend*."

"Ooooh," Lexi says.

"Nice," Nora says.

"And he felt guilty enough that he decided he should just bail on you," Charlotte continues. "When you see him again, he'll be all apologetic about it, but he'll say he can't risk what he has with Lindsey even if yes, he's very attracted to you. And that you should stop thinking about him and go have fun with your friends."

"Brava," Lexi says.

"I'm glad you're all having fun at my expense," I say.

Lexi pinches my thigh. "Lighten up, birthday girl."

Nora says, "What was so great about him anyway?"

I shrug it off. "You wouldn't understand."

"*What* wouldn't I understand?" Nora snaps.

Surprised by her tone, I calmly say, "I just mean you haven't liked anyone in forever."

She looks madder than seems logical. It's a fact that she hasn't expressed any interest in anyone at school or elsewhere in like a year or more.

"Sorry," I say. "I didn't mean anything by it."

Lexi says, "Yeah, she didn't mean anything by it," and I'm not sure why she felt the need to repeat what I'd just said except that it's possible my "sorry" sounded like "not sorry."

"And anyway," I say. "It's impossible to explain, isn't it? Why anyone likes anyone or anything? You just do."

"You're saying that you're not responsible for who you like?" Nora asks.

"Yeah," I say. "I guess? I mean it's either there or it isn't, right?"

The Aquarius Deck DJ picks that exact moment to play a song by Elvis Moriello, this British singer-songwriter that Paul worshipped and introduced me to. It's like I've got something lodged in my throat; I can't swallow, can't breathe.

We loved this song.

The album it was on was our soundtrack when we'd make out in Paul's basement or car.

I really don't want to hear it right now.

Not here.

Not now.

Not ever.

I adjust my necklace in case it's that, but it's not.

The song goes on and on and it's wrenching.

How do you give yourself the Heimlich again?

But it turns out the choking feeling is me realizing that I don't even *like* this song, let alone love it.

It's me realizing I don't actually like Elvis Moriello at all.

And if that's true, what other lies have I been telling myself?

~~~

I can't just sit here any longer. He's not coming. I ask if anyone wants to hit the shops, and Lexi says, "Sure. I'm getting fried anyway."

Out of nowhere, this guy near us starts to sing at the top of his lungs. He's belting out "Yellow Submarine."

Lexi and I look at each other and laugh awkwardly, as we slip our shoes on.

Then another woman joins in and then another two guys and more and there are suddenly maybe twenty people singing about how they all live in a yellow submarine and I turn to Lexi and say, "What the hell?"

She smiles. Charlotte takes out the ship's itinerary for the day.

"I guess it's a flash-mob-type thing?" I say.

Nora puts her schedule away. "Nothing on the itinerary about it."

"Maybe unofficial?" I say.

"Must be," Nora says.

I study the faces of the people singing, like actors in a musical, trying to figure out what kind of person you have to be to think it's okay to just burst into song in life. They seem somehow on autopilot, and I wonder if this kind of flash mob feels like that—like an out-of-body-type experience—and whether I'd like it.

I don't think so.

As quickly as they started, they're done and they fade back into the crowd as if it had never happened.
~~~

"That was weird," Lexi says.

"I dug it," Nora says.

~~~

He's in the tie shop—the back of his head silhouetted by a wall of silky colors. "Hold on," I say.

Lexi stops short and an older woman bangs into her and bags go flying and I help the lady as fast as I can and then walk into the shop—so many ties, all lined up in triangulated rows—and he's not there.

The suited man at the register looks curiously at me; I back out.

"What?" Lexi says.

"He was here. I saw him." I look up and down the corridor.

She sighs.

"What? I saw him!"

"I don't know, Nat," Lexi says. "I mean, I never even saw you talking to him. And I mean, are you making this up? Just to have an excuse to, I don't know, ditch us and be alone?"

"You can't be serious," I say, though it's true that I do sometimes bow out of things at home with my own meh excuses. "I'm not making him up!"

I remember the picture I tried to take of him. I get my phone out. "I'll show you."

But the picture before the one of the girls on the tube ride isn't the one I took of him.

It's a selfie he took.

He is shirtless, standing by the edge of the ship, and he's doing an old-fashioned sort of salute, two fingers to his forehead.

Does it mean hi or good-bye?
~~~

"Here." I hold out my phone to Lexi. "Look."

"That could be anybody. That could be something you pulled off Instagram."

"I'm not making him up!" I scream.

Then Lexi says, "Okay, okay. Calm down." She pulls me aside, next to the smug mannequins and their sequins. "I mean, you're doing okay, right? You're not, like, going crazy without any of us realizing it?"

"I'm fine," I say. "But I'm freaking out a little."

More like a lot, actually.

Because why did he take off his shirt there on the deck?

Why did he take the selfie for me?

Lexi sighs.

"I mean, I like him. A lot. There was, you know, chemistry. It was real. So why didn't he show up? What if he—"

"What if he *what*?"

Hypnotic pull of the water.

Inches from death.

My head is whirring; my stomach, too. "What if that *wasn't* him just now? In the shop. Because his shirt was there on the deck, where we were supposed to meet. And he made me say good-bye to him. He said he didn't realize how it would feel to be so close to death."

"What the hell, Nat?"

"I know!" I say, working hard to process it all, to have it make sense in a better way. "What if he jumped?"

She huffs annoyance.

"Why are you *annoyed*?"

"I'm *annoyed* because I want whoever you're going to like next to not be a douchewad."

"Douchewad?" I repeat.

"What." She shrugs. "It's a word."

"I'm pretty sure it's not," I say.

"Listen," she says. "He did not jump. He was just here, looking at ties. And last night he just couldn't show up for some random reason that maybe we'll never know, *or* he blew you off, and either way, it's time to get lunch." She puts an arm around my shoulders.

I very much want her to be right.

She is.

She has to be.

~~~

We circle back to grab the girls and hit a buffet. Men wielding shiny knives and wearing white chef's hats stand by carving stations where meats are lit with orange heat lamps. A raw bar is piled high with flamingo-pink shrimp and veiny oysters. There's a make-your-own pizza stand and a handful of other choices. The salad bar goes for nautical miles.

Charlotte starts with a plate of Chinese food, eats it, then goes back for a plate of just shrimp and soy sauce, then one more plate for turkey and stuffing, never mixing cuisines on a plate.

Lexi commits to one and only one section: burger, fries, pickles, that's it.

Nora makes an elaborate salad—adorned with chickpeas and Craisins and feta cheese and some kind of pink vinaigrette—then only picks at it.

I just take whatever I think looks good and don't care much about how it all goes together.
~~~

It's a miracle that we're all friends.

"I guess it's my turn, then," Nora says, pulling a red onion off her plate and setting it aside.

"Ugh," I say. I just want to know what the picture means. I don't want any more theories about what his deal is. I want answers.

"Just let her go, then we'll pick a winner and be done."

"Fine." I eat some chickpea salad.

Nora says, "His name is Jude or maybe Lennon and he's from Dallas. His parents were, like, big Beatles fans or whatever. And he's a star student and amazing soccer player and he's probably going to a big state school in Texas where he'll join a frat if he isn't already a freshman there, and he wears like a varsity letter jacket all the time and is a grade A asshole who has slept with like half the cheerleading squad."

My grip on my fork tightens along with my jaw.

"Last night he thought maybe he could get something started with you but then some other girl came along and he went off chasing her skirt, because that's just the kind of guy he is and he figured you were too nice for him anyway."

"Chasing her skirt?" Lexi asks.

"It's an expression." Nora sips her water.

I push my chair back and stand. "Why can't he just be an awesome, cool guy that I met and like and who likes me? Would that be so crazy?"

"It's just a game," Lexi says. "We didn't mean—"

I don't hear the end of the sentence over voices and sliding plates and metal spoons and ice machines all colliding in midair.

Lexi's voice punches above it as I exit the room. "Nat! Come *on*," she pleads.

She catches up to me by the elevators. "We need to get you a chill pill."

"I just want to be alone for a minute, okay?" I raise my eyebrows.

"Meet us back at the cabin?" She raises hers.

~~~

An older couple is playing cards in shade created by the ship's own structures. A woman on a lounger with a sleeping baby on her chest holds a paperback right near where he and I talked. A crew member pushes a bin of white towels through a small puddle, and the wheels leave tracks and squeak, mimicking seagulls' caws. I try to find an actual bird in the sky, but the air is lifeless.

I pick a chair and pull up the selfie. I zoom in on a mark just under his collarbone. It's a tattoo.

Amelia

Disappointment is a punch to the gut.

A girlfriend.

Has to be.

Charlotte wins.

Why did he bother with me at all?

~~~

Attention, all aboard the Pisces. *This is your captain speaking. I apologize for the inconvenience, but we need all passengers to report back to their staterooms for a cabin check and head count at three p.m., which by my watch is about thirty-five minutes from now. This process shouldn't take long, and you'll be back to your regular cruise activities in no time. So please, if you can, wrap up what you're doing and head on back to your cabins and await further instruction. We thank you for your cooperation.*

~~~

I don't think. I just go.

It's happening.

It's really happening.

Lexi's not right.

I am.

~~~

"What do you think is going on?" Nora says, twisting open a beer and handing it to me when I walk into the room. Charlotte's ordered another bucket.

Vertigo surges as the horizon tilts out the window. I sit down on the bed.

"Do not go to the crazy place, Natalie," Lexi says.

"*What* crazy place?" Nora asks.

Lexi says, "She thinks that her guy literally jumped ship. But it's not possible."

"Look." I get my phone out. "Why would he take his shirt off? Why would he take a selfie like he's saying good-bye? He actually *made me say good-bye* to him yesterday, like he knew he wasn't going to show. He talked about being inches from death."

Nora takes my phone and looks at it, hands it back.

Lexi says, "You *just* saw him in the tie shop!"

"I *think* I did," I say softly. "But now. A head count? I don't know."

Nora says, "It does all seem strange. We haven't even stopped in a port of call yet. Why would they need a head count?"

"I think I should say something," I admit. "Should I tell them about him? When they get here?"

"*I'm* going to say something, and I don't want you to get mad at me," Lexi says.

"What?" I say.

"Not your circus. Not your monkeys."

"What does *that* mean?"

"It means this is not your problem," she says. "If it's even a problem at all. He's just a guy you met *once*."

"What if he *died*?"

"What if he did?" Lexi ups her pitch. "What if it's someone else who went overboard? Either way, I say we just mind our own business—you know, keep on keeping on with the sail-a-brating—and let them figure it out. He's just a guy you met. *Once*. Twice, whatever."

"You had to be there," I say. "You don't understand."

"We've never been the kind of friends to let guys get between us," Lexi says.

"He's not getting between us," I say, but I'm reminded of the Bechdel test from film class and think we'd all fail it in a movie about the cruise so far. Too much talk about boys, for some reason, even though at home we talk about books and movies and the world and school and our families and everything else, too. All the time.

"This cruise is supposed to be about celebrating you," Lexi says. "Celebrating us. *Friends*."

"I'm sorry that I met someone, okay?" I say. "But I mean, cut me some slack. Can't you? All things considered?"

Regret is instant. It was a bad move to play the Dead Boyfriend Card with my best friends. I can see in their volley of eye rolls that they're exasperated with me. Maybe I'm exasperated with myself.

Maybe that's why that night with him mattered. Because I felt something. I felt like maybe I could, I don't know, love again.

Nora says, "I'm going to get some air. Let me know when they're here."

The balcony door makes a sucking sound when she opens it and again when she closes it, like it's drowning—gasping for air.

~~~

We went blindly down a YouTube wormhole that time when Charlotte made us look at cruise ship tour videos. We ended up watching a video that someone on board a ship made of a man clinging—unsuccessfully, as it would turn out—to a lifeboat after jumping or being pushed from his balcony. It was hard to see exactly what was happening at first, but then it became terrifyingly clear: he lost his grip and slipped away into the white-black choppers of the night sea. People screamed. Someone yelled, "You killed him!"

"Did that just really happen?" Nora said when we watched.

"Jesus Christ," Lexi said.

I felt sick that I'd watched that, sick like you feel when they play certain 9/11 footage and sick like news stories of floor collapses at weddings and bloody kids in war-torn countries. Sick with the impossibility of it all, with the reality of how small a person is. How at any second you can get struck down by a bullet or a tree; how a person can look so very tiny against the world, how each of us is nothing more than a speck.

~~~

When the knock finally comes, we hide the beers and greet a crew member who is holding some kind of scanner.

"All present and accounted for," Nora says.

He asks for our key cards and runs them through his device.

"Why are they doing this head count anyway?" I ask. My mouth is dry; my voice unsure. I should show him the picture, tell him what I think.

"Oh," the man says. "It's routine."

"Doesn't seem routine." I laugh nervously.

"I'm not at liberty to say," he says then. "Thanks for your cooperation. There will be another announcement when we're all done."

The door thuds closed.

~~~

The room's too crowded. We're getting cabin fever. Charlotte and Nora climb into their beds just to get out of the way, then Charlotte sits up and says, "Let's assume it wasn't Natalie's guy who went overboard. So who was it?"

"You mean what's his or her deal?" Nora says.

"I guess," Charlotte says. "Like, do you think they jumped or were pushed? Like, do you remember the YouTube thing?"

"Who could forget?" I say.

"I'm not sure which is worse," Lexi says.

"Well, what if he was a terrorist or something?" Nora offers. "Like his travel companion just discovered evidence of his plan to do something awful and they struggled."

"That'd be okay, I guess?" Lexi says.

"Oooh, I have a two-line movie idea," Nora says, and she sits up in her bed. "Imagine there's a girl standing by the railing of one of the decks. And she's taking video, so we're in her point of view, and she turns to a noise and it's a guy coming at her, and she says,
~~~

"You're late" and he says something like, "And you're a bitch" and he's charging at her and then we just see her camera falling, but it's clear she's falling overboard."

"It's good," Lexi says.

"Yeah, it's pretty good," Charlotte agrees.

"We could get Nate or Ben to play the guy," Nora says, lying back down.

"How would you film the falling phone?" I ask, and repeat the name *Ben* so it sticks this time.

"I don't know," Nora says. "I'll figure it out."

That should be the end of it, but I say, "I think it's kind of depressing. As a concept. And I mean, *hello*, violence against women."

"Well, it's not your movie," Nora says.

A sudden frost of tension glazes the room.

"It's also possible," Charlotte says, "I mean, returning to the game, that it was just, like, an accident. Like he—or she—had too much to drink. And somebody dared him—or her—to sit on the railing or something and then bam, gone."

I don't share any theories; I don't want to have any.

"You guys," I say. "Can you please stop?"

~~~

The announcement comes that we're free to leave our cabins, and the whole afternoon takes on a prison break kind of feel. We go roller skating. We ride bumper cars. We play Skee-Ball and pinball. Anything to shake off this feeling of dread.

These are my real guesses:

Julian.
~~~

Luke.

Steve.

I'll see him again and he'll explain the selfie and he'll have a perfect excuse for not waiting for me to come back.

Amelia will be a character from a book or movie; maybe the name of his beloved grandmother or cat.

It'll be no big deal.

I'll tell him that for a while there, I thought he'd jumped, and he'll laugh and say something funny, about how trolls are by nature quick to panic.

~~~

"Well, I find it all very upsetting," my mother is saying, when we join my parents at our dinner table. We're in the Top O' the Mast restaurant tonight. There is a big fake shipwreck by the entrance—like half a wooden boat sticking out of the floor—and huge plastic fish with bulging eyes on the walls. Where there aren't mounted fish, there are crowded, frenzied aquariums.

"What's very upsetting?" I ask.

"It's just a rumor," my father says. "No need to get everyone worked up."

"What's the rumor?" Lexi dares.

"Somebody fell overboard," my mother says. "Or jumped! That's why they needed the head count."

"Jean," my father says. "We talked about this."

"I'm sorry," she says, on the brink of tears. "It's just, I'm trying. It's just . . ." She starts crying, then uses her hands to wipe away tears—first left, then right, then left, then right—like windshield wipers. "So upsetting."
~~~

My friends all look at me. I don't know how to handle this any more than they do. I need water. It's too cold, though—mostly ice.

A bright white fish puts its lips to the front of the tank nearest us. Surely this is a fate worse than death for a fish; to be put in an aquarium *on a cruise ship*. It seems cruel.

"Do they know who it was?" Lexi asks.

My mother shakes her head. "Apparently a woman says she saw it happen? And someone left a cryptic note about it at one of the bars?"

"How do you know all this?" I ask, my teeth aching.

"People talk to me." She shrugs. "I ask questions. They answer."

Instant-nausea, like out of a packet, fills my gut. "Hey, Mom?" I say.

I saw him in the tie shop.

It had to have been him.

I repeat that like a mantra.

It *had to have been.*

Had to have been.

"Do you have that Dramamine on you?"

She wipes her nose. "Nat, we're barely moving." She grabs my father's arm. "Do you think they've stopped the boat for a search?"

I hold out a shaky hand and say, "Dramamine?" Then smile. "Anyway, Mom, I'm sure it's just a rumor."

~~~

We go to a cabaret show called "00Songs" in a massive theater with movie screens for walls.

"Ooooooh," Lexi says after the first act—a woman singing
~~~

"Skyfall." "*Double-Oh* songs! Like double-oh seven. Now I get it. I thought it was oooh-songs and was, like, wait—what?"

Charlotte smiles and pats Lexi on the head. "Not the brightest bulb on the marquee."

Lexi sticks her tongue out and pants like a happy dog for a second, then swats Charlotte's hand away. "Oh, like you are?"

The performers are men in tuxes and women in slinky dresses. Lights seem to change the very color of the air of the room. Music surrounds us from hidden speakers.

The screens never show any specific James Bond footage that I can tell, but it's all very Bond-*like*. Cobblestoned towns with hidden corners propped against a hill that rises from a turquoise sea. Rooftop views from tall towers. Infinity pools on white islands. Speedboats racing off to some glistening horizon. European cities in panorama. Skyscrapers of glass being scaled by wired spies.

There's no way it was him who went overboard.

It would mean loss upon loss, and no girl could be that unlucky.

Fantasies come in the form of two-line scripts.

~~~

EXT. A SMALL ITALIAN TOWN -- DAY

A young woman, maybe twenty-five years old--this is NATALIE--winds her way down a cobblestoned street lined with pastel-colored buildings. We hear the click of her shoes; we hear passersby speaking Italian. Rounding a corner too quickly she runs right into a young man. This is LUKE.
~~~

NATALIE (*in Italian*)

Mi scusi

The two make eye contact, hold it longer than seems normal. There is something there. But what?

LUKE

Natalie, is it you?

~~~

INT. IRISH PUB -- NIGHT

A young woman sits at a small table with a group of friends. This is NATALIE. She is happy, smiling at a story her Irish friend is telling, and yet we sense something is . . . missing.

She gets up, goes to the bar, nods at the bartender to get his attention. He is pulling a pint; indicates he'll be right over. When he comes over, she leans in.

NATALIE

Another Guinness, please.

MALE (O.S.)

Make that two.
~~~

```
Natalie turns to the voice. A young man--this
is ANDREW--is right there. They recognize each
other; share something deep. They kiss.
```

~~~

When I see him for real, relief is adrenaline.

He's watching a live game show in the Atrium. Three couples onstage are trying to pop a balloon on their spouse's lap—bouncing, squeaking, laughing. A massive anchor-shaped chandelier hangs ominously over them all and looks heavy enough to drag the whole ship down. Uproarious laughter from the crowd rises up to where I am, on a balcony one level up.

"That's him," I say to Lexi; the other girls decided to turn in, but Lexi said she felt restless and wanted to take a walk. "He's over there."

"Where?"

"Right there." Pointing across such a huge room seems futile, but I do it anyway, then get my phone out and show her the picture again so she can recognize him more easily. My hands are shaking. My pulse has quickened just like that.

She says, "Let me see that," and takes my phone. She deletes the photo.

"Why did you do that?" I snap.

"Because he's an asshole."

I grab my phone and turn back to him. He's laughing and clapping, and I think he's got some nerve. I snake through the crowd watching from the balcony and head down a long staircase, nearly falling when one of my sandals slips off my foot. From the swell
~~~

in the applause when I hit the main level, I can tell the show is ending.

"*No, no, no,*" I say under my breath.

People start to stand and stretch and talk.

"Excuse me," I say. "Sorry. So sorry."

No, no, no.

I've lost sight of him, but I keep on going anyway—too fast for how crowded it is—and I bump right into someone. "I'm *so* sorry."

"Married fifty years, these two. Fifty years. One more round of applause, folks, and thanks for coming . . ."

I reach where I think I should be just as I'm blinded by a spotlight.

By the time I blink it away, he's gone.

The room seems to spin; the Dramamine's not working.

One level up, Lexi is shaking her head like I'm a lost cause.

~~~

Life with Paul was easy, predictable. We spent afternoons watching old movies together and sitting on beaches and hanging out at his house listening to music, mostly stuff he loved that I'd never heard of. We liked going to the mall and not buying anything and doing homework together at the big wooden table in his dining room.

We went for drives and made up stories about houses we saw. We liked playing Scrabble with only words that appeared in song lyrics you could sing, which meant me losing a lot of Scrabble.

Above all, we loved going to the aquarium where we met—he'd
~~~

bought a membership—just to watch sea lions get fed and to touch the backs of cold, hard stingrays. He'd go on and on about everything he knew about each creature while I'd just marvel at the fact that he and I had found each other, had gotten so lucky, and never had to deal with not knowing who in the world was out there for us.

Lexi said we were like an old married couple from day one, but maybe I liked it that way.

We fought sometimes about his phone, but not really. He was an information junkie, so it wasn't like he was always doing something dumb on it, but still. Whenever we drove I had to hold it or put it in the glove box, because otherwise he'd be checking different apps for best routes or trying to find a place nearby where we could get a root beer float. And wherever we were, if we talked about something and ran into a question, he'd say, "If only there were a way we could look that up . . . ," and then he'd look it up.

Which was part of how he knew so much about so many things.

He'd have looked up rock-climbing lingo for me so that next time I'd know.

Next time I'd shout out, "Lowering!" and that would be that.

~~~

"Well, we saw the mystery man," Lexi says when we get back to the cabin. "So he didn't jump."

I head into the bathroom. The fan is loud but not loud enough.

Nora says, "Does she seriously think that a guy going overboard is more likely than him just blowing her off?"

~~~

INT. CRUISE SHIP ATRIUM -- NIGHT

A crowd is watching a live game show, some kind of married couples challenge. A winner is being crowned after they successfully pop a balloon between their bellies.

In the crowd a teenage girl--this is NATALIE--spies a boy. He is across the room. He is wearing a white linen shirt. She sets out in his direction. The crowd is scattering and blocking her path. She is frantically worming her way through them, keeping her eyes on that white shirt the whole time--it's like a beacon calling to her.

Finally, she reaches him, grabs his arm. He turns. Her disappointment is apparent.

BOY

Can I help you?

We see disappointment/confusion cross Natalie's face. It's not him.

NATALIE

I thought you were someone else.

THE STARLITE STARGAZER

Pisces Day 3!

Port of Call: Grand Turk

Highlights:

7:00 a.m. — Gentle stretching with Jan
8:00–9:00 a.m. — Pop-Up Pancakes Station—Boardwalk
11:00 a.m. — BINGO in the Saturn Room

2:00 p.m. — Matinee movie: *Interstellar*
3:00–5:00 p.m. — Live music in the Atrium: Rock the Boat cover band

7:00–9:00 p.m. — On the Boardwalk—Pop-Up Homemade Ice Cream Stand
8:00 p.m. — Ice sculpture contest
8:00 p.m. and 10:00 p.m. — Stars of Broadway through the Ages: Starlite Theater
9:00 p.m. — Retro video game challenge in Supernova
10:00 p.m. — How to Make Towel Animals—Supernova

A slice of new light sneaks past the thick drapes at six a.m.: I peek out and see land, and lights blurred by heavy air. The ship is docked. *That's* what's different. We're completely still.

I use the bathroom, then crawl back under the X-ray blanket and nod off again.

The next time I wake—one of the girls is up and heading to the bathroom—I have to shake off a dream about Paul.

I get up, stretch, pad back over to the drapes, and look out again. Eight seagulls perched on the balcony railing seem to be studying what little they can see of me and not in a kind way. When I pull back the curtain, they startle and take off, then adjust their flying positions, falling into formation like Jedi fighters called to some distant galaxy.

Who's Amelia?

~~~

The walk to the Grand Turk cruise center is small steps and bumping shoulders on a long pier; we're a herd. I'm tempted to moo. A tree we pass when we hit actual land is so full of small birds that it shakes with chirps.

Our bus to snorkeling doesn't leave for twenty minutes. When the crowd thins out some thanks to earlier buses, other destinations—there are pools and beaches right there at the center—my parents get coffees and we get iced teas, then we sit in hammocks near our designated pickup area.

"I dreamed about Paul last night." I set aside my tea to put sunscreen on.

"Good dream or bad dream?" Charlotte's ready to analyze.
~~~

“He was alive.” I open my sunscreen tube; it pushes coconut into the air. “Wearing a floppy sunhat.”

“In a good way or a bad way?” Lexi echoes. “Like, were you happy to see him?”

Nora seems oddly focused on her own sunscreen—she’s doing the tops of her feet supermethodically.

I’m studying the crowd, looking for him. Not Paul; the other him.

“Of course,” I say, carefully sliding sunscreen under my necklace, then across my breastbone.

But I wasn’t happy in the dream, not exactly. I was confused and hurt, and he wasn’t thrilled to see me either.

A small blue bus bumps and bounces into the nearby parking lot; we put away sunscreen and gather up our backpacks and board. Out the dusty window, the ship looks ridiculously high. No way anyone would survive a fall like that. The impact alone would kill you.

~~~

My mother got the call from Paul’s Aunt Betty. I was helping clean up our late dinner when she picked up her phone, then said, “Who?” then said, “Oh yes, hi there,” sounding odd, like she’d been caught in a lie.

She stepped out of the room and I heard, “Oh god. Oh no. Oh, no, no, no.”

Then a minute later, whispers, then, “Let us know if there’s anything we can do. Of course. Thanks for calling.”

She appeared in the kitchen like she’d just been to the makeup
~~~

trailer where she'd been done up for her part as Ghost Woman #3. Pale. Ghoulish. Bloodshot eyes.

"What is it?" I asked.

She said my father's name, with a shaky lilt of agony, and waited for him to turn from the sink, where he was washing a greasy pan. A poof of tiny bubbles lifted into the air.

"What is it?" he said, drying his hands on a dish towel.

"The traffic," she said. "The accident."

Bawling. Then turning to me:

"Honey, it was Paul."

My brain strained. Everything murky.

My words muffled and slowed—"I don't understand"—like I was talking underwater.

"He's dead, Natalie." She charged at me to pull me into a hug.

"No, but." I backed up to the oven, still warm from dinner; I had to move away; the hug would make it real. "It can't be."

"That was his aunt."

"You're sure," my father said like a statement and not a question—maybe because he didn't want an answer.

She nodded and tears dragged her makeup down from her eyes in black streaks—Sad Clown #1—the whole world warping into a fun-house mirror.

~~~

Snorkeling is 10 percent amazing and 90 percent sheer terror. Amazing because of the color of the water; the soft sand on my toes; the light lapping waves. Terror because I prefer my fish behind aquarium glass.
~~~

I am herky-jerky and panicky in the water. My lips and gums hurt from the mouthpiece, probably from clenching too hard.

I come up for a break, for air, and Nora resurfaces beside me. "You need to stop flailing around so much." She fills her mask with water, then dumps it out again. "You're scaring all the fish away."

"Sorry," I say.

"Shouldn't you take that off?" She nods at something on me, but I don't know what she could mean. "Your necklace."

My hand goes to it. "I never take it off," I say, though I do typically take it off to shower only to put it right back on before even getting dressed.

"You're not afraid you're going to lose it?" she says.

"I feel like I'm more likely to lose it if I take it off and put it back on a lot."

For reasons that were probably obvious but were sort of unclear to me, I'd become attached to the necklace in a way I'd never been with any piece of jewelry before. Also, the clasp was sort of tiny and tricky. Like a bunch of times I thought I put it on correctly only to feel it slink down my cleavage five minutes later.

Nora shrugs. I shrug. To change the subject, I simply look away. Charlotte is standing in the surf talking to that guy Shaun from rock climbing. She is smiling, laughing, at ease.

I slip back under the water after adjusting my gear yet again. But of course now, in addition to being freaked out by the fish, I'm paranoid about losing my necklace—it could sink and rust here, and never be found again.

After a handful of shimmering schools flash by, I spy one horrific eel—thick and fast—and decide I'm done. I go sit on my towel on the small beach. I shouldn't be surprised that snorkeling is not for me, but I am.

"What's up with Nora?" I ask Lexi, when she comes and sits beside me.

"What do you mean?"

I've already scanned the beach and the water; he's not here. "I mean she's acting prickly."

"You've *met* Nora, right?"

"*More* prickly," I say, then remember their overheard conversation. "What were you guys talking about the other night? Something she's having a hard time getting over or something?"

"It's not worth mentioning," Lexi says.

This is what I've been telling myself about that night at Nora's house, but I'm starting to question the logic.

Nora comes out of the water. Her bikini top can barely contain her. She adjusts her suit bottom and grabs a towel and sits beside Lexi. She says, "That. Was. Awesome."

Shaun splashes Charlotte, and her belly laugh ripples off the water like the sun.

~~~

"Surprise!"

We all jump at the voice.

"Mom!" I say. "Don't *do* that!"

Turns out, my parents booked a glass-bottom boat tour. So we pack up and line up with a bunch of families with small kids, then board this junky-looking boat with a thatch canopy. We slide into bench seats along a rail that overlooks the center bottom of the
~~~

boat, which is in fact made of glass. So far all you can see is sand and some rocks and shells.

The motor starts, and the tour guide introduces himself and lays out some rules about not standing and keeping your hands inside the boat and we're off. It doesn't take long before we're coasting over a large school of silver fish and there are delighted gasps from the children on board. Gasps from Florida Nora, too.

Below us, the ocean floor lights up. We're passing over a coral reef—like rainbows trapped in stone. It makes me think of Magic Rocks that Paul grew in his room, and how they've probably been thrown out. I'd sort of loved the way they looked like a miniature Atlantis where tiny mermaids might live.

I'm squeezed between Lexi and my mother. I can't think of the last time I've been this physically close to my mom for any length of time, and that seems weird.

"How're you doing?" she asks when the boat picks up speed.

"Good," I say, not sure what's expected of me.

"You're having fun? I mean, in spite of everything?"

"Yes, Mom. I'm having fun." It sounds more obnoxious than I mean it to, which is not at all. "I mean, yes, I am. So thank you."

She squeezes my knee, and even with her sunglasses on I can tell she is having some kind of fragile moment, so we do what we usually do and look away from each other. It's not that we're not close; it's more like since the accident we're both always trying to protect each other.

The captain cuts the engine, and the boat bucks and slows. An eel appears under the glass—*oohs* and *aahs*—and I try to determine whether it's the same eel as before, whether it's stalking me, messing with my head.

"That is so cool," Nora says, leaning closer to see.

Lexi elbows me and says, "Got ourselves a Jacqueline Cousteau over here."

"I know," I say. "Right?"

Nora doesn't look at us when she says, "Oh just eel with it."

Lexi and Charlotte laugh and I smile like I don't care but it's a joke Paul used to make and just like that I have a theory on why Nora's so prickly and why she didn't want to hear about my dream and why she's so interested in my necklace and what she's having a hard time getting over and I might throw up.

~~~

On the bus back to the ship, I'm sitting next to Lexi. I say, "Nora didn't, like, have a crush on Paul or something, did she?"

Lexi is looking out the window. It's taking her too long to answer.

I say, "You're taking too long to answer."

Finally, she says, "I really don't want to get in the middle of that."

"Too late," I say, and I turn to look at the back of Nora's head a few rows up. I stare hard, trying to get her to turn around to face me.

~~~

EXT. TROPICAL MARKETPLACE -- DAY

Four American teenage girls are shopping. They are all sunglasses and chatter and laughter. A teenage boy, PAUL, approaches one of the girls, NATALIE. He's wearing a floppy sunhat. To say she is surprised and horrified to see him is understatement.

NATALIE
I thought you were dead.

PAUL
Apparently you were mistaken.

~~~

I see him in the cruise center on our way back to the boat. He's wearing a blue T-shirt and tan shorts. I take off into a run, almost losing a flip-flop, and zigzag through the crowd. When I am close enough, I call out "Hey!" and tap him hard on the back.

He turns and looks at me like I'm a stranger.

"Hey," I repeat.

"Hey?" He's a robot again, an irritated one.

"What the hell?" I say.

"You're the one who stopped me," he says.

It takes me a second to recover. I hadn't been expecting . . . *attitude*? I say, "You blew me off. I want to know why."

Some kind of understanding crosses his face, and he shakes his head and smiles; teeth not quite as straight as I remembered, maybe, and more facial hair than it seems possible could have grown so quickly. He says, "You've obviously had the pleasure of meeting my brother."

~~~

I ended up in the second pew, behind Paul's parents and brother—wearing black and feeling like a cliché. I saw Nora and Lexi and Charlotte come in but had no idea whether it was okay to even talk to or smile at a friend so I didn't move, didn't make eye contact. I flipped through a hymnal like it was some kind of oracle and looked for a message in the first lines I saw on the page I landed on: *I danced on a Friday when the sky turned black / It's hard to dance with the devil on your back / They buried my body and they thought I'd gone / But I am the Dance and I still go on.*

I slapped the book shut and put it down. Because it was too creepy.

The priest's eulogy was cookie-cutter—and not even a cool shape, just a boring round *blah-blah-blah*. I wanted the whole thing to be over already so that Paul and I could leave, but of course that wouldn't work anymore.

He was dead.

I couldn't seem to get it through my thick skull.

His brother, Rich, got up to speak later at the cemetery, and I had high hopes he'd do better than the priest had. But then he started talking about Paul like he was maybe three years old and not seventeen and I found myself counting the number of times he used the phrase "little buddy." If it had been a drinking game, I'd have been sloshed.

When he finished, he put a hand on the casket, put his head down, closed his eyes, and started quietly, bravely crying right there in front of us all.

Near me, a young girl—no more than five—in a dress the color of dried lavender, whispered to her mom, "What's in the box?"

Her mother's hush carried a whistle on it.

Behind me somewhere, a girl who was not me—so someone whose boyfriend was *not* in the box—was sobbing so loudly that it almost sounded fake. It had to be.

I wanted the hymnal back. I wanted to try again for some kind of sign, new words to live by—because I wasn't crying and surely that meant there was something wrong with me.

I wondered if I could be different somehow, if I just applied myself.

~~~

He has the same fierce eyes; the same charming dimple; the same effect on my body—like he's somehow sending invisible electric charges at me.

"You're messing with me," I say.

He clears his throat and looks shy for a second. "I'm not."

"This better not be some kind of joke," I say.

"No joke," he says, and he shrugs apologetically, scratches his head, and starts to walk away.

I grab his arm. It feels like the same arm, and it seems like the same look of surprise that I touched him. "He was supposed to meet me the other night, but he didn't turn up, and then there was the head count on the ship and all." I'm not sure I'm making sense, but I can't seem to stop talking. "And he left this weird picture on my phone." I pause. "Did something happen to him?"

He shakes his head and exhales as he looks away.

A woman walking past has such a blazing, newborn sunburn that for a second I feel hot and cold and just plain ill on her behalf.
~~~

He looks back and says, "Trust me when I say that you're better off that he didn't turn up."

"Why would he blow me off like that?"

"Because it's what he does," he says with some annoyance, or maybe sadness.

"He said he had an *older* brother," I say, still trying to make sense of things.

He nods like he's heard this before. "Yeah, by one minute."

"When's the last time you saw him?"

I hear my name being called. My friends. My parents. "Natalie!" they're saying. "Nat! Nat!" and coming closer.

"It was nice to meet you, Natalie," he says, and he sounds genuine when he adds, "Sorry about my brother."

He disappears into the crowd, and I shout out, "Who's Amelia?" but he doesn't hear or if he does, he ignores me.

"Well?" Charlotte asks when my friends reach me. "What did he say?"

"It wasn't him," I say. "They're twins."

Nora snorts as we all fall into a line to board.

Lexi tips back her sunhat, like a starlet in a well-rehearsed scene. Her line is perfection: "Oh *brother*."

~~~

I'm first in the shower. To get out of the way after I'm dressed, I go sit out on the balcony.

We have three sets of twins in our year at school. Two sets of them are identical; the other girl/boy fraternal. But in both cases with the identical ones you can totally tell them apart once you get to know them a little. The reason the boat boys seem like impossible
~~~

replicas—apart from facial hair?—must simply be because I don't know them, have yet to see them standing side by side where differences might reveal themselves.

Nora is second to shower and joins me, wearing a floral sundress, long wet hair hanging over one shoulder. "So did he know why his brother didn't show up?" she says.

"No." I'm not sure whether I should broach the subject of Paul or any of the other things Nora and I have avoided talking about over the last year.

"And you're *sure* it wasn't him?"

"I don't think it was." I shake my head. "That would be messed up."

"So wait . . ." Nora has a small bottle of nail polish in her hand, shakes it. "If the one you saw in the shops and the Atrium was the twin, it's possible the other one actually did go overboard?"

"Yes," I say.

"Does his brother think that?" She starts applying the nail polish—stop-sign red—to her toes.

"He didn't seem concerned, no. I don't know. But I mean, what if they're wrong? What if his family's wrong? I mean, the photo he took. I can't shake it."

"Not much to be done about it," Nora says.

"That's not true," I say. "I need to report it."

"You're not serious." She pauses on a pinkie toe.

"Actually, I am." I stand.

"You mean *now*?"

"Yes," I say. "Now."

This *is* my circus.

These are *my monkeys*.

I head for the phone. I hit the button that says Guest Services because I don't know what else to do. A woman picks up.

"Hi," I say. "I need to talk to someone in, like, security or something? I met this guy the other night, and I think he may have been the one who jumped? I mean, if someone jumped and I mean, the rumors . . ."

"I'll send a security officer up to your stateroom," she says, and we hang up.

"What did you just do?" Lexi moans.

"I had to do *something*." My hands are shaking. "I can't waste the whole cruise thinking about him, so this way I get it off my chest and move on."

Even as I say it, it sounds like a lie.

Nora nods but doesn't say anything for a long minute, and I say, "What?"

"Nothing," she says, and she squeezes some excess water out of her hair with a towel. "It's just it's not always that easy, right? To control what you think about. Who you think about."

She looks away like she's said too much.

She has.

I don't call her on it, though. I don't ask about her crush. It seems weird, suddenly, that I never noticed that one of my best friends liked my boyfriend. Or had I?

~~~

INT. CATERING HALL -- NIGHT

A girl--this is NORA--is wearing a fancy dress, standing next to a cake with some lit candles,
~~~

others still waiting to be lit. Behind her, big balloons float the number 16.

Nearby, another girl--this is NATALIE--sits holding hands with her boyfriend, PAUL. The room is crowded with people, tables.

DJ

And now Paul is going to come up and light our next candle. Paul?

NATALIE

Does he mean you?

Paul raises his eyebrows, shrugs, stands up, and walks to Nora and the cake, lights a candle. She kisses him on the cheek and he returns to his seat.

Natalie takes a long drink of water.

~~~

There's an urgent knock.

Lexi opens the door.

A man in a kind of uniform I haven't seen yet stands there. He has a walkie-talkie by his shoulder. It crackles. "You called security?" he says.
~~~

I step out in front of Lexi. He says, "Are your parents around?"

"Next door," I say, and he steps back to let me pass.

I pad out into the hall barefoot and knock. My mother answers, and the officer says, "Your daughter requested we come talk to her, and I want a parent to be present for the conversation."

"Natalie," my mother says. "What's going on?"

"Can we talk in your room?" I say.

She steps back to let us in, and my father gets up off the sofa where their suitcases have detonated and blown clothes everywhere. He echoes my mom with his own "What's going on?"

"I met this guy in the teen lounge the first night," I say as we all try to shift around in the too-small room—it's like an awkward square dance—so we can stand facing one another. "We left the lounge and played shuffleboard together."

My mother makes a scoffing sound.

"And I met up with him later, too. On the Gemini Deck."

"What time was this?" the officer asks.

"Around nine. We were going to go in one of the hot tubs. But after I came down to change and went back up, he was gone."

"Natalie," my mother says. "You promised to stay with your friends."

"I know," I say. "I'm sorry."

"What was the boy's name?" the officer asks.

"I don't know. I never asked."

"Did he say anything strange?"

"Well, I mean, we were just talking and it didn't seem strange in context. But he talked about how it felt weird to be inches from death, like when we were outside by the railing, and then he made me say good-bye to him when I came down to change into my swimsuit and he took a selfie where he was kind of saluting or waving good-bye."

"Can I see the photo?"

"My friend deleted it."

"And you haven't had any other contact with him since?"

"I thought I did, but it turns out it was his twin brother?" I say, and it sounds far-fetched. But the officer seems unfazed, like he already knows there are twins involved.

"Did you see him interact with anyone else on the ship?" he asks.

"No, I don't think so."

"Didn't see him talk to anyone? Even a casual interaction?"

I shake my head. These seem like weird questions.

He says, "Well, if you think of anything else, let me know. And thanks for coming forward." He turns to my parents. "Thanks for your time. I'm sorry for the trouble."

"Wait," my mother says. "So the head count? It came back wrong?" She steadies herself by grabbing my father's arm with both her hands.

"No, ma'am. The head count matches the manifest. Nonetheless there have been multiple suggestions that someone went overboard, so we need to follow up and try to root out the source of the confusion."

"Of course," she says.

He leaves and they turn to me and I cut them off. "I know," I say. "I'm sorry. I should've stayed with my friends. I promise I'll do better."

My mother is about to rip into me; sharp words are forming on her lips.

But my father says, "Natalie, we really just want this to be a fun and relaxing week. A reset button, you know? For us all. So we're letting this slide, but if you'll forgive the expression, we need you fully on board."

~~~

"Well, that was weird," I say to the girls. Everyone's dressed for dinner, and the room smells of a bad mix of shampoos—seaweed and strawberries.

"How so?"

"They wanted to know if he was behaving strangely, and like if I saw him talking to anyone. But they said the head count was fine, that it matched the manifest. But there were other people saying someone went overboard."

There's another knock at the cabin door.

My parents are incapable of being even a minute late to dinner.

~~~

I rediscover an old skill in the Libra Room, where the chandeliers all take the shape of the Libra scales. I wash food down with big swigs of water. I look to achieve a perfect balance of food on my plate, like a Libran might, then rearrange it all to make it look like I've eaten more than I have.

My mother seems cheered by the good news about the head count. But I can't shake the feeling that something's wrong.

Heads start to turn around us—toward some kind of commotion by the dining room's main aisle. A woman, maybe twenty years old, in a long silver dress, is pointing. The room quiets enough that we can hear.

"Don't you see it?" she says to a waiter who approaches her. "It's right there!"

"I don't see anything, miss."

"There's a glass floating right there." She reaches for this supposed glass and finds only air, loses her balance, falls into the waiter's arms. Then she sees that everyone is looking at her, staring, whispering. "Don't you see it? It's right there!"

The maître d' comes over to assist, and tries to take her by the arm. "Miss, if you'll please—"

"Get your hands off me!" she screams. Then she walks proudly out of the room. When she's gone, chatter rises and silverware is taken up again and the noise of the room swells until it's full.

"She must be drunk," my mother says, like that's the final word on it.

My father drains his cocktail, holds his glass high to order another.

~~~

I excuse myself to go to the bathroom. Lexi comes, too.

The girl who saw the floating glass is in there, throwing water on her face. I want to ask her if she's okay, but I catch Lexi's eye and she just raises her brows and disappears into a stall. I do the same.

When we come out, the girl is gone. As we wash hands, Lexi says, "I'm sorry, but this cruise just keeps getting weirder and weirder."

"Agreed," I say, and reach for a paper towel.

~~~

He's standing outside the Libra Room.

He could be either twin. He shoves his hands in his pockets, then takes them out again. "Can we talk?"

I study his body and feel a sort of heightened awareness of my own. "Which one are you?"

"I'm Michael," he says. "You called security? About my brother."

"Yeah, well, you didn't seem too concerned about him, so I thought someone should be." Of course it all seems a bit much now that I know the head count was correct.

"Can we talk somewhere?" He looks around. "Somewhere *else*. I won't take a lot of your time. Please?"

"How did you find me?"

"I noticed you and your friends last night. I figured we were on the same dining schedule."

I want to walk away.

Set the big top on fire and shut the whole circus down.

But I can't shake the image of his brother. That salute. The Amelia tattoo. Who is she? And, if he didn't jump, where is he?

"I just want to ask you a few questions," Michael says. "Because I haven't, you know, seen him, since that first night either."

Lexi, who has been waiting close by, is out of patience. "So you're the twin," she says.

"Well, I'm Michael," he says. "We're both 'the twin.'"

"What's the other one's name?" she asks.

"Ray."

She reaches over and twirls my ponytail in her hand; for a second it tickles my neck. "Well, when you see *Ray*, can you tell him he's a douchewad?"

"Nothing I haven't told him before," Michael says, and Lexi lets a smile slip.

"Lex?" I say. "I got this, okay?"

She fades back into the dining room, and I turn back to Michael. He runs a hand through his hair, leaving the front of it arguably worse off but somehow cuter.

Yes, he's cute, too.

Of course he is.

Possibly even cuter, though without them side by side, it's hard to say for sure.

"I wasn't going to bother you," he says. "And I'm sure he's fine and that you shouldn't worry—like *at all*—but I really need to find him and I just want to know what you guys did, what you talked about in case it helps me. That's all."

"Sure," I say. "Of course." I see my parents coming toward me. "Gemini Deck at nine?"

"Thank you thank you." He clasps his hands together in gratitude, and then he takes a few backward steps away from me and then turns and heads down the corridor. I watch until he turns a corner, out of sight.

~~~

"What are you doing, Nat?" Lexi says, while we wait for the elevator that will deliver us to the ice sculpture competition. My parents have decided on a show instead.

"Nothing," I say. "What are *you* doing?"

"I'm not getting involved with random drama on a cruise ship, that's what I'm doing."

"I'm not *getting* involved," I point out. "I'm already involved."
~~~

The first elevator to arrive is the glass one. After we get in and go down a few levels, we're looking out at the Atrium. I scan the crowd as we drop and stop and drop and stop.

"But you can be *less* involved," Lexi says.

Charlotte and Nora are both mute; they do this sometimes when Lexi and I are in a thing. They just seem to glaze over like they don't hear us at all.

"I just want to see him again, okay?" A woman walks into the Atrium to the delight of her children and husband. The children, two girls, run to her. "I need to know why he blew me off. And I want to know who Amelia is."

"Who's Amelia?"

"He has a tattoo. Ray, the first one. It says Amelia."

"Why do you *care*?" Lexi presses.

I care because I lost someone, and maybe he did, too—maybe it was a grandmother, or even just a cat—and maybe that explains part of why I felt such an instant bond with him. But I don't want to say that. I resent being pushed.

I say, "I just do! Why does anyone want anything?"

The doors open and Charlotte and Nora step out, maybe wishing they didn't even know us. When Lexi and I go to get off, a family that is too eager to get on has to stop and back out of our way, like a parting of the seas.

~~~

The evening drags on. I should've told him to meet me earlier.

One man with a small chain saw carves an old pirate ship with tall sails out of a block of ice; the other makes a castle. The pirate ship wins with louder applause.
~~~

We stop at a homemade ice cream stand on the Boardwalk. The flavors are aggressively quirky, like with basil and sweet corn. I get cilantro and lime and don't love it, but my stomach's off from nerves so who knows.

We ride the small carousel; it's just four of us and that seems somehow fitting and also dumb. Nora opts for a chariot-like bench with King Triton's face painted in glittery colors. I'm on a gray dolphin behind Lexi, who's on a yellow sea horse, who's behind Charlotte, who's on a clown fish. When we get off I feel dizzy and stay away from the ship's rails, because one man-overboard scare per cruise is probably plenty.

Lexi realizes she's lost her key card, so we retrace our steps but then end up at the guest services desk; they make her a new one.

We head to Supernova for a retro video game challenge. Lexi's the only female contestant. She aces all these games I've never even seen, never knew she could play. In her last round, it's a game like Crossy Roads, only it's a frog trying to cross a busy highway and then some rivers packed with floating logs and snapping crocodiles.

I watch as an overly pixelated alligator eats her final frog alive.

Lexi groans but she ends up taking second place anyway.

Nate takes third.

The first-prize winner is Charlotte's pal Shaun, and she high-fives him; their hands seem to magnetize for a minute.

I slip out.

~~~
~~~

INT. CRUISE SHIP CABIN -- DAY

A teenage girl--this is NATALIE--stands by the window. Birds are gathering ominously on the railing. She turns, exits the room with a shawl wrapped dramatically around her shoulders.

INT. CRUISE SHIP HALLWAY -- DAY

Natalie walks down the hall; the ship is lilting, making it hard for her to walk straight. She punches an elevator button, gets in.

INT. ELEVATOR -- DAY

She's alone. The numbers light up so very slowly.

EXT. CRUISE SHIP DECK -- DAY

Natalie arrives on an empty deck. Empty but for a crew member who is mopping up some kind of red liquid. Blood? Strawberry daiquiri? She goes to the rails, pulls her shawl closer. A boy approaches and she turns when she hears him. Studies him.

NATALIE

```
You have to tell me who Amelia is.
```

BOY

```
No, I don't.
```

~~~

He's waiting for me, sitting on the edge of a lounge chair. He stands as soon as he sees me. "Hey, thanks for coming."

"Sure," I say.

"Let's talk over here," he says, and he leads me to two cushy armchairs near where I believed I was falling in love with his brother. Nearby, there's a big stack of the same loungers Ray and I sat on, and I wonder which ones are the exact ones, wonder how long they held our heat.

"I was hoping you'd just run me through how you met my brother, what he said, everything." Michael's eyes are alive with curiosity.

"I don't know how to do that," I say. "I mean, we sort of covered a lot of ground pretty quickly."

"Oh, now I get it," he says, and an emotion I can't quite read—disappointment? envy?—darts through his features.

I take a moment to study him in detail—full lips, dark lashes, sleeves rolled up to reveal light brown hair on muscular arms. I say, "Get what?"

"You like him."

"I didn't say that." There's a vein in his arm that's so distracting; it makes him somehow too real.
~~~

"Didn't have to." He half smiles. "But anyway, that's neither here nor there. So would you just tell me the basics? Please?"

I tell him about the teen lounge. Vodka. My sail-a-bration.

I tell him about the opposite of here.

I tell him about shuffleboard and my dead boyfriend.

"Oh god, I'm so sorry," Michael interrupts at that. "That's awful. I'm so sorry."

I say, "Well, it's not like you killed him, so you don't have to be sorry."

He says, "You know what I mean."

I nod.

"I mean, like, are you okay?" he asks.

I nod again, less sure this time.

We're quiet against the loud ship and ocean and world. Then I tell him about being near the edge of death, and the hot tub idea, and how his brother made me say good-bye and called me dollface.

"And you said something about a picture?"

"It looked like he was saying good-bye—sort of waving or saluting? And he'd taken his shirt off. I'd show you but my friend deleted it."

"Did he talk to anyone else that you saw?" His eyes are now deep pools of interest. "When you were together?"

"No. Why do people keep asking me that?"

"He didn't ask you to do anything odd?" A flat pebble of concern skims through his gaze.

I shake my head, "No," and the ripples settle when he blinks.

He nods and stands. "I really appreciate your taking the time to talk to me, so thanks. You may now resume your sail-a-bration."

I stand, too, reluctantly—wanting for him to ask me to stay, wanting him to ask me more questions so that maybe my own answers will help me better understand what I felt for his brother and what I'm feeling now—and how they're the same or different.

But I'm the one with the question. I say, "Who's Amelia?"

He looks oddly devastated, then his whole body tenses, like preparing for impact. "Why? What did he say?"

"Nothing," I say. "In the photo, I saw his tattoo."

"You should go," he says. "You should just forget you ever met him. Okay?"

I say, "Tell me who she is and I'll go."

"You need to *forget about him*." He sounds a little unhinged now. "And if you see him, seriously, do not talk to him. Just walk away."

"Why?" I have to fight an urge to cry creeping up inside me. "You're scaring me."

"See this?" He reaches for a braided string bracelet on his left wrist. It looks old, soft, delicate. "I never take it off. You see one of us, you make sure you see this, because then you know it's me. If you don't see it here, it's not me. And you walk away. You don't listen to a word he says, you don't make eye contact. You walk away and you find me or you go back to your parents or friends. You do not engage."

"Okay . . . ," I say slowly, my hand going to my neck. My necklace.

"Promise me you won't talk to him," he says, and it sounds like an irrationally desperate plea, considering we barely know each other.

"Okay," I say. "I promise."

We stand there staring at each other and he steps closer and for a second I sense menace emanating from him but then his body softens and he moves closer still and he shakes his head and says, "I just can't tell you more. I'm *so sorry*."

Behind us voices rise up. "That's him there!" a man in a Mets cap shouts.

Two cruise employees approach and say, "You're going to have to come with us" to Michael.

"What's going on?" Michael says.

"Just come with us."

"Why?" he pleads.

"We'll explain in the office," one of them says.

Michael looks at me—"Thanks again, Natalie"—then nods at the men.

As they escort him away, one of them says, "Miss, you really shouldn't be out here alone."

His words are a smack.

I want to tell him that it's a weird thing to say.

I want to tell that man that I should be able to be wherever I want to be.

Even though I'm a girl.

Even though I'm alone.

What does he think is going to happen to me, exactly?

If someone had warned me about Nora's party, would I have gone anyway?

I nod and feel a sharp despair peck at me, like some bird of prey is snacking on my heart.

Even out here, in the middle of the ocean, nothing's really different.

Wherever you go, there you are.

~~~

I find my friends in Supernova. They're learning how to make towel animals. I join in. Anything to take my mind off the twins, off Michael's bizarre words of warning.

"Soooo? How'd it go?" Lexi asks.

I take a towel and try to start a turtle. "He told me to forget I ever met his brother."

The instructor is going too fast. If you miss a step, you're screwed.

"Sounds like good advice to me," Lexi says, folding her towel the wrong way.

"He said it in a weird way, though." A long fold now and then a quick flip, some rolling. "Like if you see him, whatever you do, don't talk to him. Just walk away."

Lexi's turtle shell crumbles in on itself. She says, "Ack!"

"He said it like his brother is . . . dangerous," I clarify, twisting a towel corner into a turtle leg.

She shrugs. "Maybe he is."

I've met dangerous boys before. The kind of boy that doesn't respect. Doesn't see girls as more than their bodies. Doesn't take no for an answer; doesn't think he has to even ask a question in the first place.

That night at Nora's.

"You don't think he, like, hurt her? Amelia? Like maybe killed her, even?"

"He'd be in jail, Natalie."

"Yeah," I say, "of course."

Miraculously, my turtle actually looks like a turtle.
~~~

I go get a drink and study the stack of glasses, imagine one of them floating in midair.

"Hey," Ben says; he's getting water, too. "Your turtle came out awesome."

"Thanks," I say, and we walk back to the demo. Elephants are up next; I reluctantly shake out my turtle.

The security officer I talked to appears in my line of vision.

"We need to talk," he says. I step away from the group with a towel in my hand.

"We went back to the surveillance video of the Gemini Deck when you claim you were there with Ray Haines. It shows you putting a bar tab on the bar."

"Yes?"

Ray Haines. It sounds made up, and he's starting to feel that way, too, as hours and days tick by.

"Care to explain?" the officer says.

"Explain what?" I say. "I already told you I met him there that night. I didn't drink any alcohol, if that's what you're—"

"The *note*. Can you explain the note?"

"What note?"

He holds it out for me to read:

"Hearing good. Eyesight adequate. You're it, lady."

"I don't understand," I say. "What does it mean?"

"Well, since it was written with quotation marks we figured it was a quote, so we looked it up. It's from an old TV show. An Alfred Hitchcock show about a man who jumps off a boat to try to slow it down and win a bet about how many miles the ship could travel in one day."

"I still don't understand." Where's Mr. Cassidy when I need him? He'd told me to look up a TV show episode, but I never followed up.

Did Ray quote Hitchcock just for me?

"This note is part of what caused the whole head count panic. So do you want to tell us what's actually going on?"

"I have no idea!"

He gives me his best Condescending Older Man look, but I don't fall for it.

"Listen," I say. "He obviously played me. I don't know why or what the whole thing is about, but I didn't have anything to do with it. I thought I was putting his check on the bar. I thought I was being responsible coming to you with information I thought might be important."

He seems stuck,—like he wants to tell me not to go anywhere for a few days—*ha*—in case he has more questions. He says, instead, "Well, let me know if you think of anything else."

~~~

It's the first night we're having anything that qualifies as "weather." Wind. Clouds. Serious swells. Occasional outbursts of lashing rain. It's hard to walk a straight line down the corridor at bedtime. We look drunk—like *rah-rah* party girls—even though we're not. Rain and seawater cling to the ship's windows, obscuring the night—the world—from view. I want very badly to be able to see some point very far in the distance, but it's no use.

When we go back to the cabin the bed has four towel animals on it. An elephant has a single red rose curled in its trunk beside a note: *For Natalie.*
~~~

"What the hell?" Nora says.

No one else has a note or a rose.

I go to the door and look out into the corridor to see if Bonny's around, but he's not. He must have had a hand in this?

"That's just creepy," Nora says.

"Is it supposed to be some kind of apology?" I say.

"Which one is it even from?" Charlotte asks.

I assume Ray—he asked my stateroom number that first night, when we were parting ways—but . . . "I'm actually not sure."

"Which one do you *want* it to be from?" Nora asks.

It's an uncomfortable question. Maybe not even worth answering.

"I'm too tired to think straight," I say, even though it's not really true.

I go into the bathroom with the shower, where my toothbrush is. They haven't asked about what Michael and I talked about or what the security officer wanted, and I haven't told them.

One thing has changed, though.

I'm not just confused anymore.

I'm angry.

~~~

I wake sweaty from a dream.

In it, the picture on the stateroom wall came to life. The ship was moving out of the frame, and the people on the beach all turned to me and had black holes for eyes.

~~~

```
INT. CRUISE SHIP DINING ROOM -- NIGHT
A woman in a long flowing dress--ghostlike
```

in her appearance--is pointing at the air. A crowd is watching, midbite.

WOMAN

Don't you see that floating glass?

MAN

There is no floating glass, miss.

~~~

EXT. CRUISE SHIP DECK -- NIGHT

Two teens, NATALIE and RAY, are alone with the night sky. Stars everywhere; shooting ones, even.

RAY

You making wishes?

NATALIE

I wish I'd never met you.
~~~

★ THE STARLITE STARGAZER ★

Pisces Day 4!

Port of Call: Nassau, Bahamas

Highlights:

7:00 a.m. — Wake-Up Zumba with Carol (Gemini Deck)
12:00–2:00 p.m. — Bahamian Buffet on the Boardwalk

Movie matinee: *Galaxy Quest*

5:00–7:00 p.m. — The Conch Outs Live Band/Aquarius Deck
8:00 p.m. — Songs about Sailing Sing-Along in the Piano Lounge (Atrium)
9:00 p.m. — Karaoke in the Supernova Lounge
10:00 p.m. — New Wave Dance Party
11:00 p.m. — Live Piano "Name that Tune" with Lenny Lancaster

The weather cleared overnight, or we've sailed out of it. Maybe both. The sky is so blue that it looks fake, like it must be green-screened behind the port.

I think about coming down with some kind of sickness to get out of spending the day at The Reef resort. Haven't I done an excellent job of avoiding the tube ride? Shouldn't I be allowed to just sit and relax?

Plus, the ship will be emptier with so many people getting off to explore Nassau. It will be easier to find Michael and find out what last night was all about; and harder for Ray to hide from me if that's what he's doing. Why would he want people to think someone went overboard?

But there is no getting out of it.

And probably the brothers are getting off, too.

Bonny and his cart of linens are there on our way out. He's full of cheer, wide smiles. "You got your gift from your admirer, yes?"

"Yes," I say, feeling icky about the whole thing. "Did he say anything to you about it? About me?"

"No, he just said he knew your birthday was coming?"

"Tomorrow, yes."

"Yes, he wasn't sure. It's okay? He knew your cabin number, so I figured you must have given it to him."

"Of course." There's no point in explaining.

"Everything okay?" my mom asks when she sees me talking to Bonny.

"Yup!" I say. "Everything's great!"

~~~
~~~

We moo our way through another busy marketplace. Women holding laminated pictures of braided hairstyles ask us if we want our hair done. When we don't, they ask us again and again; one woman even shoves aside a competitor. They're most interested in Charlotte, whose hair is loose and curly today, a way she never wears it at home. Two stylists start bickering about who saw her first, and Charlotte backs away and says, "Maybe later, sorry!"

Local men are shouting about scooter rentals and haggling with some guys from the ship who say they only want Yamahas. I feel foolish for having pictured little-kid scooters and not the motorcycle kind.

Thoughts pop up in my crowded head like protest signs:

YAMAHA OR BUST!

What do we want?
HAIR BRAIDS!
When do we want them?
MAYBE LATER?!

WE DEMAND THE TRUTH ABOUT AMELIA!

DOWN WITH RAY!

We board a small bus, and it lurches through a congested downtown area. Slick high-end stores like Fendi and Cartier look out of place on the ground floors of chipping pastel buildings. Overstuffed gift shops spit T-shirts and key chains onto the sidewalks. We pick up speed outside town, past a blur of small houses, then go over a bridge toward shining crystal resorts, like giant Magic Rocks.

We check in as day visitors in the resort's main lobby—where a massive tank of coral and fish rises up from the ground. With bracelets now on our wrists, we head through a set of doors with nose-to-nose dolphins etched into glass. The pool area is flowering bushes and winding pathways and pools you could use to teach a preschooler shapes—round, square, diamond, oval, rectangle.

We grab towels and find chairs, apply sunscreen and kick off shoes.

We splay ourselves over squeaky tubes and take a few trips around a lazy river, which is totally my speed but would be more my speed without the bridge where you potentially have a bucket of water dumped on you. Each time I pass under it, I tense but get lucky.

We swim half-hearted laps in a pool with a waterfall that makes it almost too loud to talk. We don't bother trying.

We take a long walk through a cool, wet tunnel of aquarium tanks. A sea turtle sails into view and seems to study me. I'm in that human aquarium Paul and I joked about; the plaque reads: *Female American Teenager. Often moody and discontented. DO NOT FEED.*

Lexi and Nora brave some of the more terrifying slides—one of them a sixty-foot drop at a near ninety-degree angle. I have to close my eyes, even as I am trying to take a video of Lexi's first plummet. My stomach leaves my body for a second, in sympathy.

I'm still a secret service agent, scanning the crowd for him—no, them—but with slightly less focus and urgency; like I'm off duty.

After lunch at a restaurant inside a cave by the pools, my parents spring their big trap of a birthday present: a dolphin encounter.

They tell my friends I've been asking to do it since I was little, but I think they have me confused with someone else. Also, how do they not know that dolphin encounters aren't even supposed to be a thing anymore? That most resorts are shutting them down.

The dolphin is named Delphine; her skin looks and feels too tight, too fleshy, and her calls sound strained, painful. No one else seems bothered; maybe I have an earache.

I smile through it and my parents snap photos. If they had any idea how much and how often I fake things for their benefit, their hearts would break.

I think about pithy things I'll say to Ray; maybe I'll lie and say I never turned up for hot tubbing anyway.

I catch myself in a daydream about Michael and try to shut it down, but then I just go with it.

I wouldn't dare share my confused emotions with my friends; no one's interested. And maybe even I have begun to sense that no, this is not something I should be involved in.

We bump into Nate and Leo and Ben, and all move to the beach area. Lexi and Nate head for the water with some boogie boards, and it's like the rest of us aren't even there. I watch them in the water together, and the chemistry seems to light the water around them like phosphorescent fish would.

Leo settles into a lounge chair beside me and starts asking me things about home and school. He's really sweet and just normal and upfront. He's easy to talk to and he keeps trying to loop Nora into the conversation but she seems determined not to participate.

He tells a joke that genuinely cracks me up—"What do you call a nose with no body?" "No-body knows!"—then we talk a bit about the weirdness of the cruise.

"So after all that, it turns out the head count was right, but there are still rumors," I say.

"How do you know all this?"

"Oh," I say. "My parents have been really staying on track of it, I guess?"

"I heard it was a woman," he says. "Blond and naked."

"That's so weird," I say. "I think I actually heard that, too, but didn't know that's what they were talking about."

If I'd known it was a woman who supposedly went over, maybe I wouldn't have gotten so worked up.

When Leo gets up to go in the water, he asks me if I want to go, but I decline.

"Nora? What about you?" he says.

"Not right now, thanks."

He shrugs his disappointment at me, and I shrug back.

"Hey," I say to her when he's far enough away. "Why don't you go in the water with him?"

"Why didn't you?"

"He likes you," I say.

"Hadn't noticed," she says.

Then she's quiet, with her eyes closed in the sun. I catch eyes with Charlotte, and we also share a shrug. I have no idea why I'm trying to match-make. I guess if she liked someone new, it would make it feel less weird that she liked my boyfriend?

Lexi comes back and dries off and puts a hat on. "Come on, birthday girl. I've got a surprise for you, too."

"Oh, jeez. What now?"

"There's a guy doing caricature and portrait art over there."

"Not really my thing," I say.

"Not up to you," she says. "It's a birthday present."

"Seriously?"

"Seriously." She slides her flip-flops on. I do the same.

"You coming?" Lexi says to Nora.

"I'm good," Nora says.

Charlotte, meanwhile, has run down to the water. She and Leo both jump over a wave. Cruise Charlotte has eaten Home Charlotte whole; not a single crumb on the plate.

~~~

Lexi gets thirsty and bored watching the artist draw my portrait—I said no way to a caricature—so I tell her to go get a bottle of water. I end up staring at a wall of goofy exaggerated faces, playing What's Amelia's Deal? in my head.

She's beyond loaded. Her dad is some kind of visual artist who grew up in the military, and now he owns a plane he flies just for fun. Her mother came from money and has never worked a day in her life and mostly manages her husband's image and career and manages Amelia, too—like takes her to get birth control and mani/pedis. They own multiple houses that they've named things like Hill House or The Lookout. Amelia met Ray at a cousin's lavish wedding. It was love at first sight—they danced to "Shout!" together—and now they're talking about going to the same small college somewhere in the Northeast. She designed the tattoo.

No, scratch that.

She's in a roller derby league. She's . . . Amelia Tearheart.
~~~

She has a ton of brothers so grew up on skateboards and talking smack. She's tougher than Ray is, and he likes it.

She's hot. Like off the charts. A daredevil, too. And probably damaged. Or dead.

Definitely dead. You don't get a girl's name tattooed on you when you're a teenager unless the girl is dead.

Car accident?

Rare cancer?

Some kind of freak infection from soil that soaked into an open wound, barely a scratch?

Lexi is back with water; she hands me a bottle and I shut down the game.

"He got escorted away by some security officer yesterday," I say. "Michael, I mean. What do you think that's about?"

"I think that's just one more sign that these guys are bad news."

"You've liked people that I thought were bad news before."

"Name one."

"Luke Jacoby."

"Oh yeah." She drains the rest of her water in one long go, licks her lips, puts the cap on the bottle, and tosses it into a nearby recycling bin. "And you know what? You were right!"

"To be honest," I say, "I don't always like the way Jason talks to you."

"Yeah, well," she says. "Join the club."

"But why do you put up with it?"

"We all put up with stuff," she says, and I'm about to ask her what she means, exactly, when she says, "Nate has a girlfriend, in case you were wondering."

"I wasn't."

"Anyway, we're not going to, like, cheat. In case you were wondering."

"I wasn't."

"Anyway, he's cool. I like him. As a friend, I mean."

"Good," I say. "I'm glad."

Charlotte joins us just as we get a first glimpse of my portrait.

"It's perfect," Lexi says.

"Yeah, it's pretty good," Charlotte says.

But I don't think it looks much like me; maybe more like my twin if I had one.

We walk back toward the beach and pass a hair-braiding stand. Charlotte approaches the woman and talks to her, then takes the chair. The woman goes to work on her, giving her row upon row of tiny braids, and I sit with her and watch the transformation. I think about telling her about the note Ray tricked me into leaving for the bartender—how I'm angry about being some pawn in his game—but Charlotte looks so relaxed there in the chair and I don't want to spoil it. Her eyes drop closed while the stylist's fingers do quick, machinelike work.

"You look amazing," I say when Charlotte's hair is done.

"Thanks." She studies herself in a hand mirror. "I could never do this at home."

"Why not?" I ask, but I feel like I know, too, that kids at school would give her a hard time and I'm not sure why but it's true. I know exactly who it would be—Tanya Benson—and what she'd say: "Where'd that cruise go? Africa?"

Charlotte just gives me a look, like, *Do I really need to explain?*

"Well, you look great," I say. "You always do."

~~~

Back down on our hall, Bonny is still making up rooms. "Your friend, he came by. He left a message for you. A stateroom number." He hands me a piece of paper.

"Did he say anything else?" I ask.

Bonny says, "He said he just wanted to explain."

I turn and start off in the direction of 10502. It's clear on the opposite side of the ship to where I am. Couldn't be any farther if it was intentional.

I've somehow figured the ship out without even realizing it. I know exactly which elevator gets me closest, which hall to turn down, which decks to avoid to get there most efficiently.

Maps are for losers.

~~~

INT. CRUISE SHIP HALLWAY -- DAY

A girl--this is NATALIE--races down the hall, clearly on a mission. She hits an elevator button again and again. Then decides instead to take the stairs. She pushes past a young boy doing some kind of waving of a card in front of a moving digital painting.

INT. CRUISE SHIP HALLWAY -- DAY

Another hallway. She consults a slip of paper in her hand. Looks at signs about which cabins are which way. Heads off to the right with new commitment.

Finally, she knocks on a door. A boy opens it. Natalie reaches for his arm, sees a bracelet there.

NATALIE
Michael.

MICHAEL
Were you hoping it would be my brother?

~~~

INT. CRUISE SHIP HALLWAY -- DAY

A girl--this is NATALIE--races down the hall, clearly on a mission. She hits an elevator button again and again. Then decides instead to take the stairs. She pushes past a young boy doing some kind of waving of a card in front of a moving digital painting.

INT. CRUISE SHIP HALLWAY -- DAY

Another hallway. She consults a slip of paper in her hand. Looks at signs about which cabins
~~~

are which way. Heads off to the right with new commitment.

Finally, she knocks on a door. A boy opens it. Natalie reaches for his arm, lifts it. She's looking for something. But what? She reaches up for his shirt collar, pushes it aside. There's a tattoo there that reads: Amelia.

NATALIE

Ray?

RAY

Were you hoping it would be my brother?

~~~

When I knock, there's movement in the stateroom, then nothing.

I knock again.

He opens the door and looks apologetic and says, "Thanks for coming. I just wanted to explain. About last night. So you didn't have the wrong idea about me. But I didn't want to, like, stalk you or whatever."

"Okay," I say.

Last night.

Bracelet on his wrist.

Michael.

For a second I'm not sure if I'm relieved or disappointed. For a second I'm annoyed at both of them.
~~~

"Someone said I'd stolen their wallet. And I didn't. *Obviously.*" He seems to realize we're standing in the hall, and he says, "Do you want to come in for a second?"

I ignore the question. "Why would they think that?"

"It had to have been my brother. So I explained that, and they seemed to believe me. My parents vouched for me."

"Why would he do that to you?"

"Like I said, he likes to mess with people. Most often me. And I'm really sorry he dragged you into this. But I'll leave you alone now and hopefully he will, too."

I know for sure now who the rose was from. And no, he's not leaving me alone. "He had a rose delivered to my room last night."

"Did you see him?" he asks, sounding panicked.

I shake my head.

"Good."

"*You* still haven't seen him?" I say.

"No," he says.

"But how is that even possible?" I say. "Aren't you, like, sharing this room?"

He shakes his head. "He only agreed to come if he had his own space. So my parents got us our own staterooms."

"Isn't that incredibly expensive?"

"It's not a problem for us."

"Well, couldn't you stake out his stateroom, then?"

"It may come to that," he says. "But he's right next door"—he points—"and I haven't heard him."

"But he had to have been back for the head count," I say.

"Or he figured out a way around it," he says. "Tricked someone or paid someone. But he wasn't next door. Anyway, Natalie, I just wanted to explain about last night. I wanted you to know I didn't do anything wrong."

"Why do you care what I think?" I ask.

"I don't know," he says. "I just do."

And I swear there's something in his eyes that's saying more, straining to be heard even in the silence.

"What if I want to help? Find him, I mean."

"I really don't think—" He trails off, like maybe he's unconvinced of it himself.

"I'm tired of people disappearing on me." I push past him into his stateroom; it smells like candy apples.

"Your boyfriend didn't disappear," he says, letting the door close. "He died."

"It feels the same."

"My brother's not worth your energy."

"But he's worth yours?"

"I'm stuck with him. You're not."

"Well, you're stuck with me now, too. Because he got me involved in whatever game he's playing."

"Natalie," he says.

"Don't 'Natalie' me," I say. "You don't even know me."

He's quiet for a second, studying me.

Then he says, softly, "I think I'd want to. Know you, I mean. If things were different. But they're not."

His honesty is disarming. I want to stay focused. And maybe I want to know him, too. Or maybe I'm confusing this with the spark I felt with Ray that first night. Maybe I don't care.

I say, "He asked me to put his bill on the bar and I did it. But it wasn't a bill. It was a cryptic note from some Hitchcock show about a guy who jumps off a boat."

He sits and sighs and rubs his eyes. The knees peeking out from under his shorts are bony and boyish.

"I want to know why he's doing this and why he got me involved."

"Listen, Natalie. I didn't want to have to say this, but I *have* seen him. And he told me he met a girl that first night but that she seemed too intense and maybe too clingy because her boyfriend was dead so he blew her off." He looks at me with defiant eyes. "And the reason he hasn't had to sleep in his cabin is because he's, you know, a player. So just move on. He just wasn't into you."

"You're lying," I say, and tilt my head involuntarily. I don't know how I know it, but I do.

"Sorry if none of this is what you want to hear," he says, and he shrugs a sort of dopey shrug.

"You're a terrible actor," I say, and my hands form fists. "Anyway, they're going to have to find him. They're going to have to get him to explain."

"You're not listening."

"I am, too—"

He sounds like he's joined the Exasperated with Natalie Club when he says, "According to a security officer I spoke to today, my brother said he had no idea what that note was about; doesn't know you; wasn't there. My guess is he's not on the surveillance footage that you're on at all. Anything he's up to, he'll deny and people will believe him. And the other woman who claims she saw someone go overboard? They have no link to him on that, like making her say that or anything. She's convinced she saw a blond woman fall off. So it clearly wasn't Ray if that's what you were worried about."

"But why would he want everyone to think someone went overboard? It's a horrible thing to do."

"He's very specifically trying to get back at me and my parents for something."

"For what?"

"I can't get into it." He strides over to the door, opens it.

"That's it?"

He gives me a long look and I think for a second that he's going to tell me everything but then he just shakes his head, steps out into the hall, and lets the door close, leaving me in his cabin.

I catch the door before it latches, open it, follow him down the hall.

He's walking impossibly fast. I almost lose him when he slides into the glass elevator, but I'm able to stick an arm out. The doors beep and bounce open.

I get in and just stare at him as we start to go up and up and up.

He says, "Do you ever wish that this was all just over with?"

"The cruise you mean?"

"No," he says. "I mean, yes, no, all of it. All of this just not knowing what your actual life is going to be like, where you'll end up, whether you'll ever be happy."

"Well, yeah," I say. "All the time. Doesn't everybody?"

"Not everybody I know," he says. "Not *anybody* I know, honestly."

"I'm going to find him." I step up to him, and even though he's so very tall I don't feel small.

He reaches out and puts a hand on each of my upper arms and squeezes the tiniest bit. He says, "I'm asking you not to."

"Why can't we just find him together?" I ask.

He shakes his head no, and it's a no that seems to be answering more, bigger questions than the one I've asked. It's a nod full of regret. The kind of no that he wishes were a yes. He lets go of me.

The doors open and he shows no signs of movement.

I'm done here.

I step into the hall and say, "You know how to find me if you change your mind."

~~~

On the Aquarius Deck, I duck at a flash of color. A beach ball soars past. A dripping man chases after it—"Sorry!"—picks it up, and sends it flying back to the pool. For a second I'm surprised you're allowed to have beach balls on a cruise ship. What if it had flown too far and gone in, maybe ended up in the belly of a whale or choking a sea turtle?

Ah.

Of *course* the woman who went overboard was blond.

And naked.

It was Ray's girlfriend.

She's inflatable.

~~~

The Starlite Room—the last of the four we'll see before we rotate back to the beginning—has a roaring-twenties-swing-club vibe. It's all black and white and gray and mirrored, and there are art deco posters on the walls. A swing band in a far corner is playing standards. I imagine this is what dining rooms looked like on some of the first luxury cruise liners—ones named after queens and that crossed the Atlantic in epic fashion—and I guess that's the point.

The food and drinks are all retro stylized, too. Oysters Rockefeller. Waldorf salad. Bathtub punch.

Across the room I spot the woman who'd seen the floating glass, and she looks perfectly, well, sane.

A new kind of peace and confidence settles over me, like a shawl.

I know his name; I know his cabin number—Michael's minus two.

I have a few tricks up my sleeve, as well.

~~~

I head for the flower shop. I buy a single rose. I go back to the cabin and, sure enough, Bonny is there with his cart, doing turn-down service. I go into my stateroom and write my note on the small Starlite notebook on the desk.

Back out in the hall, I approach Bonny. "Hey, can you do something for me?"

"Of course!"

"That guy who left the rose for me? I want to return the favor. I have a note for him, and this? If I give you his stateroom number, can you get it to his stateroom?"

"Shouldn't be a problem," he says.

~~~

We shoot a two-line movie. One written by Nora, who has ditched her other idea. She directs. Lexi and I star. We're two friends stuck in an elevator.

The problem with shooting it is that people keep calling the elevator so the doors close and we move, so we have to stand up and pretend we're not doing what we're doing.

We need one clean take with no other people needing the elevator for maybe thirty seconds.

After a couple of old people ride down exactly one floor—"How lazy can you get?" Lexi says—we try again.

Charlotte holds the elevator's door-open button, keeping watch.

Lexi and I sit on the floor and scatter some candy wrappers, like we've been here a while.

Nora holds up her phone and says, "Action."

I stare up at the ceiling while Lexi roots around through her purse. I deliver my line—"No one's coming, and we're both going to die in here."

Then Lexi stands and says, "You idiot, you just forgot to press the button." She hits a button.

"And cut!" Nora says, just as some perplexed-looking people arrive to use the elevator.

Lexi and I stand and collect our props. We all pile out into the hall, giggling.

~~~

I imagine, again and again, what his face will look like when he sees my note.

He'll read it, and it'll take him a moment to get the reference. But if he's familiar enough with Hitchcock TV shows to quote one, he's surely seen *Rear Window*. He'll know that the words I wrote were the same as the note the main character, Jeff, has delivered to the man across the courtyard. Jeff is convinced his neighbor has killed his own wife and disposed of her in pieces.
~~~

It says:
"WHAT HAVE YOU DONE WITH HER?"

~~~

I picture her floating toward a tiny island with a single palm tree. She'll make a nice life for herself there, maybe with a quirky crab for company.

~~~

EXT. CRUISE SHIP DECK -- NIGHT

Calm seas. A teenage girl--this is NATALIE--stands looking out at the water, her dress flapping lightly in the breeze. Behind her, a teenage boy--MICHAEL--comes through a set of doors. He steps up behind her. She senses him there but doesn't move.

MICHAEL
I've been looking everywhere for you.

NATALIE (*turning*)
Well, you found me.

~~~

Karaoke has never been my thing. Shocker. Tonight, I don't mind being able to hide in a room where it's happening. I listen. I clap. I know the drill.
~~~

One girl sings "Part of Your World" from *The Little Mermaid*, and she's excellent, but I imagine those mom whales rolling their big whale eyes and thinking, *Not this one again*.

Charlotte decides to get up and sing the theme from *Ghostbusters*. Lexi and Nate and Leo join in, and it's hilariously bad.

At the entrance, Michael appears. My body is a first responder and places an urgent call out for backup from my brain.

I'm way too happy to see him.

I hadn't been expecting that.

I'm not even sure what it means that he's here.

He's wearing shorts and a hoodie, with his hands in his pocket, and comes in looking shy. I wave and he waves, then he looks at the karaoke action and I get the feeling he's going to turn around and walk right out; maybe, like his brother, try to find the opposite of here.

I point toward a more tucked-away lounge area, and he nods and starts off in that direction. I go that way, too, and we meet by a set of red leather chairs. The music is more muted here, at least.

"Hey," I say.

"Hey," he says.

"Any sign of Ray?" I ask, not sure whether I'm ready to share my inflatable doll theory yet.

"Can we talk about something else?" he says, with a sort of weary desperation. "Literally *anything* else? Just for a little while?"

"Of course," I say. "Sure." We're both quiet, looking over to the karaoke stage, and then I laugh and say, "Um, like what?" right as he says, "Sure is nice weather we're having."

A smile drifts between us.

"I got nothing," I say.

He goes to stand up and says, "Guess I'll go," then smiles and sits back down again.

"Have you ever been on a cruise before?" I ask.

"Nice," he says. "A good conversational softball." He nods and says, "As a matter of fact, I have. And it was a much more interesting one than this. I mean, well, never mind. It was just more . . . educational . . . for lack of a better word."

"Educational is *better*?"

"Well, I mean, it was to cooler places. Colombia and Costa Rica—these crazy islands called the San Blas Islands. And the ship actually went through the Panama Canal locks. So that was cool."

"If you say so," I say.

"I got to hold a sloth," he says.

"What was *that* like?" I ask.

"It was, er, damp." He smiles. "I basically never wore the shirt again because it reeked of sloth."

I laugh.

"Not a metaphor. It literally reeked of sloth. I washed it a bunch of times but then just threw it out."

"I got you."

"The people of San Blas make their living mostly through tourism, which is depressing. Like, sure, take a picture of me with my sloth but give me a dollar, you know? But the place is incredible. They have different islands for different needs. Like there's an island that's sort of designated for . . . see now, I've talked myself into an awkward corner."

"You can say it," I say when I get his meaning.

"I'm not sure I can." He makes a funny wincing face.

"Sex," I say. "It's okay. I've, you know, heard of it."

"Maybe we *should* talk about Ray," he says.

"Too late," I say, though I feel the awkwardness, too. If this were a screenplay, Mr. Cassidy would tell me that the scene is boring, that it needs action. We should be playing Ping-Pong or, at least, walking or eating, so that there'd be room for subtext and symbolism. But even with the strangeness of it—of us just sitting and talking; no phones, nothing to do with our bodies, our hands—I don't want it to stop. I say, "So you travel a lot?"

"I do, I guess, yeah. My parents. It's sort of like their thing." He seems to start to relax.

"Where are you even from?"

"Florida," he says.

"Where in Florida?"

"Brandon," he says. "You?"

"Clearwater," I say.

It's weird to think they live close enough that our schools' sports teams probably compete with one another in regional tournaments.

I ask, "What's your favorite place you've been?"

"Hawaii," he says without blinking.

"You didn't even have to think," I say.

"It's like you've gone to a different planet entirely. I loved that. We took a helicopter ride over an active volcano. I mean, I also loved Italy—the food was just ridiculous, and I mean, riding a gondola in Venice is a trip. And I love Ireland—just all that green and the music and the people. But still, Hawaii."

"You're so lucky," I say. "My parents are not remotely adventurous. At all."

"Well, pretty soon you can go wherever you want to."

I smile. "You paying?"

"You'll have your own money eventually. Where will you go?"

"I've never really thought about it."

He leans toward me and says, "What about college? Staying in state?"

"That's the plan," I say.

"Don't sound so excited," he says. "Isn't there *somewhere* else you want to go?"

I say, "There's always somewhere else I want to go, but when I get there I always want to leave."

"That can't be true." He laughs.

"It is!" I laugh back.

"You just haven't been to the right place yet."

"So I spin a globe and stick a finger out and see where I land?"

"There's no place calling you? No inkling?"

"I don't know." I think hard. "I've always thought I'd like New Orleans, but I have no basis in reality."

"It's such a great place."

"Have you been *everywhere*?"

"Working on it," he says.

"Where do *you* want to go to school?"

"DC, if all goes according to plan. I want to study international relations, and there are some great programs."

That's the difference. If Ray comes off as some kind of reincarnated movie star, his brother is maybe some kind of war hero taking another turn. He's probably spent his whole life as a kind of diplomat, maybe apologizing for his brother, covering his tracks, cleaning up messes.

Over on the stage, a kid who looks a lot like Justin Bieber gets up and actually sings a Bieber song. I say, "Cruises are weird."

He says, "Can we get out of here?"

This time, with this brother, I don't hesitate.

I say yes.

~~~

"Cruises remove everything that's actually cool about traveling," Michael says as we walk out of Supernova and down the corridor that leads you out and up to the Boardwalk Deck.

"What do you mean?" I ask as we step out into hot wind.

"Being a tourist is a little bit uncomfortable, you know?" He's careful to hold the door for me. "You have to navigate a new place and try to fit in with local customs. You eat different foods. So you learn something about how to be, like, in the world, right? But on a cruise, *everyone*'s a tourist. So in a way no one's a tourist. You know what I mean?"

"I never thought of it that way, but yeah, I see it. Because it feels like we're away but also like we're not."

"Exactly. Of course, *you* have your friends with you."

I nod. "Yes, I do."

"Seems like a lot of togetherness," he says. "I can't imagine doing that with my friends."

"It is. *A lot.* But it's good. Everyone's, you know, trying so hard. For me. For my sake, you know?" It sinks in closer to my core how hard my parents have worked to try to make things better for me. "My parents—" I trail off and shake my head.

"They lost something, too."

I nod, not sure of his meaning but not able to speak.
~~~

He says, "They lost a version of you that hadn't lived through it."

I nod and push back tears.

It hasn't been hard because he, Paul, wasn't next in line to die. It's been hard because when he died the world changed and I changed with it.

We're walking past the balloon water gun race, and the guy running it says, "Step on up! Everyone's a winner."

I look at Michael and raise my eyebrows, and he shrugs. We each slide onto a small stool and pick up a water gun. Right then a young girl and her mom also grab guns down at the other end of the stall.

"And a ready-set, and here we go!" the guy says, and a bell rings and the guns in our hands come alive.

I find my clown's mouth and shoot water right in. "I wasn't sure I was going to see you again."

I maybe hadn't realized how badly I wanted to.

"I wasn't sure either." He sounds superserious for a second; his aim isn't as good as mine. "Can I be honest with you?"

"I expect you to be."

He turns away from his clown to look at me—I can see him in my periphery—when he says, "I sort of can't stop thinking about you." The water from his gun is going all the wrong places.

"Why?" I half laugh; a defense mechanism; my gun dips and I have to find the clown mouth again.

"Can't explain it," he says, and he turns back to the game and aims his gun at my clown.

"Quit it," I say, and I nudge him and lose my own aim again.

Me. Neither.

The mom wins. Of course she does. Her daughter picks a

stuffed stingray—purple wing-fins with details in gold thread—and Michael says, "Excellent choice."

We find chairs and sit without talking. Michael's leaning forward, with his elbows on his knees, and he's playing with his string bracelet with his right hand. He's just spinning it around on his wrist, and I realize I very much want to reach out and hold his hand. There's no point denying something is happening.

"Did you make it?" I ask. "The bracelet?"

"No," he says, and he stands. "How is it still so hot out?"

I hadn't noticed.

He unzips his hoodie and peels it off. Beneath it, a white linen shirt. Short sleeves.

My expression must shift because he says, "What's wrong?"

I say, "Your brother was wearing a shirt just like that when I met him."

"We share similar taste in clothes if nothing else." He sits back down.

"Take it off," I say, with an edge.

"What?" He looks at me like I must be crazy or joking. "No."

"Take it off," I repeat, questioning everything about bracelets and facial hair and the straightness of teeth and every way I thought I could tell them apart. "I want to make sure you don't have an Amelia tattoo. I need to look at the shirt and see if my lip gloss is on it."

"Are you serious?"

"I am."

He has the nerve to look mad at me. "Why would your *lip gloss* be on my brother's shirt?"

The deck seems to be slipping away from me, like a wave

receding at my feet. He's starting to unbutton his shirt, and I feel sick with anticipation. I say, "I'm not even sure there are two of you at this point."

He stops unbuttoning and shoots me this look of disappointment, then stands. "I knew this was a bad idea."

"*What* was?"

"Liking you." He shakes his head, as if disapproving of himself or maybe just me. "Because if you honestly can't tell the difference between me and my brother, then I don't want to be here anyway."

"You'd rather just *leave* than prove to me who you are?"

He answers by walking away and not looking back.

~~~

I struggle to tame confusion, pulling it into some manageable shape, like cotton candy on a stick.

One shirt, or two?

One boy, or two?

How can I be sure?

I head for the guest services desk—four floors down, midship.

The elevator is empty, unmotivated. So very slow. Maybe I actually wouldn't mind being stuck here for a while. Because I'm actually pretty sure people don't really die in elevators anymore. If they ever did. But I won't tell Nora that; that her whole premise is flawed.

A couple with two young boys gets on, each parent carrying a sleeping child. "We overdid it," the woman says, like she needs to explain.

I'm not sure I've ever overdone anything—at least not before this week, this moment. Maybe the reason I'm so scared of the ship's heights is because my whole life to this point has been flat.
~~~

There's no line at guest services. The man behind the desk asks me how he can help me.

"I'm wondering if you have a lost and found? I'm looking for a shirt? It's a men's white linen short-sleeved shirt. It's my brother's."

"We have a bin but I haven't logged everything in a few days," he says. "You're welcome to look through it, though."

"That'd be great," I say.

He goes to the end of the counter and opens a short swinging door and gestures at the clear plastic bin.

"Thanks," I say.

I kneel down and start to rummage. Some pale blue cat's-eye sunglasses I'm tempted to take. A book called *The Woman in Cabin 10*, about a murder on a cruise ship, which seems a weird pick for someone to have brought along. A pink shawl. And there, under it, a men's white linen button-down shirt. Short sleeves. My lip gloss on it.

Two shirts.

Two boys.

Too late.

"This is the one," I say, taking it with me because I sort of have to, to keep up my fib. "Thanks."

I head back toward Supernova and leave the shirt on a porthole sill on a long corridor when no one's looking. Apparently, my imaginary brother loses stuff all the time.

~~~

Back in the lounge, I'm dragged up to the stage to sing "Girls Just Want to Have Fun" with my friends.

But it's not true.
~~~

Girls don't just want to have fun, not always.

I didn't that night at Nora's.

I don't right now.

Afterward, I tell the girls that I'm heading back.

I think about finding him, apologizing.

But if he's so dead set on not letting me in, I won't let him in either.

Teeth get brushed. Pajamas get put on. Almost by invisible hands controlling me.

Not my circus or monkeys after all.

I crash hard.

~~~

I dream I am walking across a high skinny bridge. It's crowded enough that people are walking single file. Then suddenly there's no one ahead of me except a young girl, maybe nine years old. She takes a wrong step and she falls and, impossibly, her body spins flat like a record the whole way down before landing with a thud.

It's only when I climb down off the bridge that I see that it's a younger version of myself lying there dead.

I wake in a cold sweat, kick off the thick blankets, and take purposely deep breaths until my heartbeat calms and my skin dries.

Nora's grinding her teeth, like she's eating chalk.

I hear the ship's engine cut out.

I check the clock.

Two a.m.

My birthday.
~~~

★THE STARLITE STARGAZER★

Pisces Day 5! Are we having fun yet???

Port of Call: STARLITE COVE!

Highlights:

On the Pisces:

7:00 a.m. — Wake-Up Zumba
11:00 a.m. — Bridge tournament in the Saturn Room

1:00 p.m. — Water aerobics, first come first served
3:00 p.m. — Matinee Movie: *The Fault in Our Stars*
7:00 p.m. — Newlywed Game—Atrium
8:00 p.m. and 10:00 p.m. — Improv comedy troupe *That's What She Said* takes over the Starlite Theater (18 and up)

On the island:

9:00 a.m. — Snorkeling lesson
9:00 a.m. — Bike rental station open
9:00 a.m. — Light hike. Meet by the entrance to the first beach.

1:00 p.m. — DINO DIG in the sandbox at the KidZone

10:00 p.m. — Fireworks on the Aquarius Deck

When I wake up again, everyone else is still dead asleep. I find a copy of the *Stargazer*, slid under the door, then I slip out onto the balcony. The air holds a cool mist and smells unmistakably of *land*—as distinct as the smell of fish food or blood.

I sit.

I feel older, or maybe just calm.

My phone won't be buzzing all day with people wishing me a happy birthday. I won't be taking or posting birthday selfies.

I noticed a birthdays section in the *Stargazer*. I look for it now.

Happy birthday to Angie, Matt W, Lester B, and Natalie!

I put the paper down and tuck my knees up under my nightgown and watch the day form. It starts out hazy, out of focus, then the lens clears.

I wonder whether Ray is plotting some response to my note.

I wonder whether Michael feels sick and sad about it all, the way I do—whether he even cares that it's my birthday.

~~~

The girls pull small gifts from hidden pockets of suitcases like magicians. From Lexi, a small clear tote that holds a dozen perfume sample wipes, all with funky names like Secret Genius and Wild Child and Garden Gangster and Tambourine Dreamer.

From Charlotte, something called a Mini Cinema Lightbox. It's a small white box light with letters and numbers you can slide in to make little signs like a movie marquee.

Nora's is last and smallest, like a box for jewelry.

"You guys are so sweet," I say as I rip off the paper. "You really didn't have to do this."

The paper comes away to reveal a small white box.
~~~

I open it and see my initial *N* in a funky font on a shiny circular pendant on a delicate sort of metal rope. I lift it out. "This is so cool," I say. "I love it."

"Put it on," she says, and for a second I go to do just that, but then I hesitate.

"I will," I say. "Later."

That choking sensation again—a heavy chain of emotion suddenly tugging at me. Links of anger and more. She knows what the necklace I'm wearing means to me and that it has to do with Paul.

"Thanks so much, guys," I say, to move things along. "All of you. You're the best friends ever."

~~~

We have a quick breakfast with my parents, who've signed up for some kind of low-impact hiking excursion on the island, then pack up day bags and disembark. Just beside the ship, Starlite has left out bug repellent and Zika warnings. I haven't missed bugs, that's for sure. I Deet-up and wonder how things worked out for that ladybug back in Miami.

Next we pass a cruise photographer, who positions us near a large anchor prop; the ship looms behind us. We smile, then "go crazy" for a second shot.

The island is a long curved strip of beaches that form a small bay.

At the first beach along the path, Lexi says, "Let's keep going."

"Why?" Nora asks.

"People are lazy." Lexi doesn't even stop. "Especially people who are on cruises. It'll be less crowded."
~~~

She charges on; we follow—past a big barbecue hut and picnic tables; past a small souvenir shop; past a tube and float rental stand, and beverage stations and fresh fruit buffets.

The second beach is, in fact, less crowded—at least so far. We pick a spot near the water in the shade of some dwarf palm trees. There are two chairs per umbrella so Lexi and I grab one pair and Nora and Charlotte the other.

"I'm already frying," Lexi says, taking out still more sunscreen and putting a hat on.

I head for the water and start to wade in. Sharp shells scrape my feet, like a warning. Beaches are fun and games, but the ocean itself is a horror show and I better not forget it.

The water is bright turquoise around me but gets darker along a clear line about fifty feet out. I feel strangely drawn to it, wondering if the water drops off and gets much deeper there, so I push forward, and the water inches up around my waist.

It turns out it's seaweed. I back up some—eels could hide there?—and turn to face the shore. Hundreds upon hundreds of chairs and umbrellas lined up neatly along the beach. Some mom types have dragged chairs to the water and sit half-submersed, while their children play, completely oblivious to the fact that the ocean could kill them and might. A toddler girl cries—seawater in her eyes.

I miss my parents.

When I get back to the chairs, we're down one.

"Where's Nora?"

"Went for a walk," Charlotte says, without opening her eyes.

~~~
~~~

When Nora still isn't back an hour later, Lexi starts to get nervous. I admit I'm a bit nervous, too. Maybe it's because we've been put on high alert due to the cruise's bizarre circumstances, but my mind goes directly to some kind of tragic fate.

We set out to find her, heading farther into the island since Lexi saw her go that way. All the while I'm looking for them, too.

But mostly him.

Michael.

Something bad has happened to Nora.

I'm sure of it.

~~~

EXT. TROPICAL ISLAND -- DAY

A teenage girl, NORA, walks obliviously down a path. A menacing-looking man appears from a connecting path and starts to follow her. When they turn a corner, they're alone between high shrubs. He seizes an opportunity, puts a hand over her mouth and drags her off the path. When he removes his hand to better hold her:

NORA

What do you want?

MAN

Just cooperate and you'll live.

~~~

EXT. TROPICAL ISLAND -- DAY

A teenage girl--this is NATALIE--walks down a beach path, clearly looking for someone. Around a bend, a boy--RAY--appears. They share a look; there is history of some kind there.

RAY

You're going to want to come with me if you want her to live.

NATALIE (*bluffing*)

You've obviously mistaken me for someone who cares.

~~~

We don't find her after scanning the next two beaches, so we double back—coated in sweat and irritation.

Nora's in her lounge chair and looks up. "Where *were* you guys?"

"Looking for *you*," I say.

"Where were *you*?" Lexi says.

"I took a walk," Nora says. "*Like I said I was going to*?"

"We were worried," I say.

"Well, you shouldn't have been," Nora says.

Charlotte says, "Anyway, we're all together now!"

Then everyone high-dives into silence. It seriously feels like a competition—who can be the most quiet and irritated for the longest, who can score a ten for the most elaborate righteous indignation with the smallest splash.
~~~

After a while, Nora surfaces and says, "I saw one of your twins."

"Which one?"

"Not sure," she says.

"What was he doing?" I try to sound aloof and fail.

"He was in the water at the next beach down." Then after a quick dip back into that deep silence, she says, "Talking to some girls."

My face gets so hot it's almost cold. Why is she trying to hurt me? Because I'm daring to try to move on?

"Did you notice if he had a tattoo?" I ask, because who cares what she thinks of me anyway. "Or was wearing a sort of rope bracelet?"

She tilts her head, like she's re-creating the scene, and says, "Pretty sure both."

Which can't be right.

I clap a mosquito dead.

~~~

After a barbecue lunch at a big buffet, I decide to be the one to take a walk. But I make a promise that I'll be back in no more than half an hour. They know where I'm going and why. I don't care.

When I spot one of them, he's talking but I can't see to whom. My angle's all wrong; there's a palm tree in the way. I don't want him to see me, not until I can try to figure out which one it is.

I have to walk a few more feet and wait for some people to pass before I can find a better vantage point. He takes a few steps backward around the same time, and his companion comes into view.

His twin.

They're together.

I reel.
~~~

They're laughing. Like the joke's on me.

I can't spot a bracelet on either one of them, and their backs are to me so I can't see which one has the tattoo.

I head for them, but there are so many chairs and people and umbrellas that I can't walk a straight line. I have to weave through the beach crowd, and each time I look up to see where I am in relationship to the lifeguard stand where they're standing, I'm turned around. It's like the game show in the Atrium again, only worse. Because of burning sand and hot-hot sun and a more high-pitched anger in my gut.

By the time I get free of the chairs and loop over to where I saw them, they're both gone.

I put a hand to my forehead like a visor—my sunglasses aren't doing the job—but I can't see either of them anywhere. There are too many bodies; too many bare chests. I do my best methodic sweep of the beach, but the suspects remain at large.

I head back to the girls and take my seat in silence.

"Did you find them?" Lexi asks.

I say, "Nope," just as sunscreen finds a sweat channel right into my eye. It stings.

~~~

We know the drill. We stop at the hand sanitizer station by the gangplank. We put our bags on the belt for the metal detector. The air-conditioning in the Atrium hits us like an iceberg.

Nora and Lexi figure the line for the tube ride will be shorter than usual, so head there. "It's a really mellow ride," Lexi says to me. "Not scary at all."

"I'm going to go shower," I say.
~~~

"I'm just peeking into Supernova for a minute," Charlotte says. "Shaun said he'd be there. Then I'm going to shower, too."

"It's really fun," Lexi says to me. "You sure?"

"I'm good," I say.

Nora looks away and I know she's rolling her eyes, but seriously.

It's a *tube ride on a cruise ship.*

It's not like it's a Venetian gondola or the Panama Canal.

~~~

I step on the note slipped under the door.

Happy birthday, Dollface.

Hitchcock always said blondes make the best victims.

My sense of self inflates.

I'm right about the doll.

So I know *how* he did it but not *why.*

~~~

The horn sounds and we're off again. We watch from our balcony as we back out of the port and then slowly turn toward the open seas. On our way out we pass a small lighthouse on a tiny barrier island. I wish I could somehow be there and not here. I wish I could climb its winding staircase up to the top and turn on a light, like a beacon, and announce, "Here. Here I am."

Like a warning.

Once we gain speed, the ship's waves are reflected in the glass of the captain's bridge and it looks like the whole glass chamber is filling with bright white smoke. But it's only an illusion.

We get ready for dinner—I put the necklace from Nora on along with the one I'm already wearing.

Bonny wishes me a happy birthday.

The meal goes exactly how I feared it would.

~~~

INT. CRUISE SHIP DINING HALL -- NIGHT

The room is gardens and fountains. Lights like stars overhead.

Waiters gather around a table with a lit piece of cake.

They are singing "Happy Birthday" to a girl, NATALIE, who is smiling awkwardly while the candle burns and burns. When the song ends, her companions--MOM and DAD, we assume, and a few friends--clap.

MOM

Well, go on and make a wish.

NATALIE

I wish you'd listened to me when I said "no singing."

~~~

Lexi booked the escape room. It's the four of us plus Ben, Leo, Nate, and Shaun and we get locked into a room midship on a lower deck; the belly of the beast. For a second I think about levels of trapped; how if the boat started to sink, other people might survive—just jump from decks and swim to lifeboats—but not us. It makes it seem more essential to me than I would have guessed that we try to solve the mystery and get out.

It's a Clue-like murder mystery set in an old hotel. The room is set up to look like a hotel lobby and a video plays on a monitor, presenting our mission: to find out who killed a guest named Ava. They give us a short list of suspects. Ben takes notes on the whiteboard.

There's a key in a mailbox behind the desk, so we open it and find a note for Ava. It's in the mailbox for room 204. It says: "*Meet me at the bar at 9 p.m.*"

"Wait," I say. "There's another message here on the desk for the same person. It says, '*Ava. I waited an hour. Call me—Alex.*' "

A door on the far side of the room says "204," but it's locked.

"How do we get in there?" Nate asks.

The monitor is now counting down the hour we have to figure this out.

We scour the room for clues and revisit what we know about our suspects. The hotel owner. The bartender. Alex. Ava's ex-husband.

Shaun finds a plastic card, like a room key, on the floor behind a fake plant and waves it in front of the door marked 204.

The lock beeps.

He opens the door.

It's a guest room. Some strewn possessions. A light on the phone is lit, so Charlotte picks it up. "Voice mail," she says.

It's from a woman named Ellen. She says, "Got your message. I'm on my way. I have what you need."

We add Ellen to our list of suspects.

I'm tasked with hunting through the drawers of the bureau, looking for clues. I find a glove that has a key in it, and it opens a desk drawer. There's a flashlight in there. But it has no batteries.

Nate and Ben think we should be looking for clues as to motive, that that will help us figure it out. They want to think big picture. I'm thinking small.

I go back to the drawers, pulling them out and turning them around, and find a battery taped to the back of one.

Nora finds a key in a suitcase, and everyone starts trying to figure out what it might open.

Behind a painting, I find a safe in the wall.

We need a four-digit code to open it.

Shaun finds a magnet on a string in a coat pocket.

Nora holds up a notepad where there's the faintest impression of some numbers. She reads them off. I punch them in on the safe keypad, and it clicks open.

Inside, there is an envelope. And a massive pile of fake cash. Also a small locked box.

"Who would want to kill her for the money?" Ben asks, and he goes back to our list of suspects and what little we know of them.

Lexi puts the batteries in the flashlight as I read the note in the envelope aloud.

"*To Whom it May Concern. I have reason to believe my life is in danger, and if you find this letter, it means that I had good reason. I dare not name any names for fear of repercussions for my family. But I hope that the truth will one day come to light.*"

Leo finds a printout of a map that gives directions to a pier.

There is some sand in the shoes by the door to the room. So our victim definitely made it to that pier and back.

She had a bar tab that was closed at 8:50 p.m. Right before she was supposed to meet Alex.

"I still have this magnet, and no idea what it's for," Shaun says.

Everyone decides to focus on that, looking over every inch of the room again.

We're going in circles.

It's making my head hurt.

Nate studies a small statue of a cat, but it's just a statue.

Then I find a small key in the bottom of a vase and Shaun says, "Aha!" and uses the magnet to retrieve it with steady hands. But the key doesn't open the small box we found in the safe.

"Maybe we missed something," I say, "in the first room."

So I go back to the lobby. Shaun comes. Charlotte, too.

"This is fun," Shaun says to her as they look through the mailboxes again.

"Yes," she says. "It is."

"There has to be a clue in that note," I say to no one in particular. "Something about the flashlight? And the truth coming to light?"

I study all the papers on the front desk. One of them is just a blank piece of paper, which seems weird.

I head back to the other room to get the flashlight.

"Nooooo," Lexi says, watching our final seconds tick away.

A loud buzzer mocks us.

The door swings open. And just like that—released—I don't really care about the mystery anymore at all.

~~~
~~~

We pour out of the room and onto the nearest deck and grab chairs by one of the snack stands. Some of the guys get burgers, and Ben sits across from me with his. "It's going to drive me bonkers that we didn't figure it out," he says.

I think I'm already over it.

"That's a cool necklace," he says. "The one with the bar. Is it like map coordinates?"

"Yup," I say.

"Where for?"

"Oh, just a place that, you know, means something to me."

"Why? What kind of place?"

"You know what? I'm starving for some reason." I get up and go order some pizza. It's not his fault. Still.

Nora's talking to Ben now, with her back to me while I wait for my slice, then it arrives. Charlotte and Shaun are talking and laughing, bemoaning our inability to escape in time. "You pulled your weight, at least," Charlotte says.

Shaun says, "I try."

"I was kind of useless," she says.

"You're too hard on yourself," he says.

Right as I'm about to take my seat, Nora says, "Sometimes I want to rip it off her neck."

"Wow," I say, putting my pizza down. "Tell us how you really feel."

She turns.

I say, "Why do you care so much about my necklace?"

"You really want to do this now?" In spite of her words, she looks eager for it.

"Do *what*?" I guess I want her to start it.

She steps away from the boys, and I follow.

She whirls around at me. "You wear it like some kind of trophy or prize or something. Like you guys are still together or like pledged forever even though you're ridiculously obsessed with these twins."

"Why do you care?"

She looks away like she's gathering energy and then says, "Because he *was going to break up with you*, Natalie! It was over. He just never had the chance to tell you."

"He was going to be with you. Is that it?"

"Yes. He was going to be with me." She starts crying and wiping away tears, and it's like I have no idea who she is anymore. "I mean, he was on his way to tell you when he—"

~~~

EXT. CEMETERY -- DAY

A small gathering, an older teen--RICH--is beside the casket, eyes closed. Crying. Nearby, a teenage girl--this is NATALIE--sits stoically, like embarrassed for him.

A young girl in a lavender dress leans over to her mother.

GIRL
(*whispering*)
What's in the box?
~~~

Her mother shushes her. Elsewhere, another teen--this is NORA--starts sobbing. She's at the back of the group, inconsolable, even as her friends--LEXI and CHARLOTTE--try to calm her. It's no use.

LEXI

(*to Charlotte*)

We have to get her out of here.

~~~

"I'm sorry." More fake-sounding sobs. "I never wanted to tell you that, but it doesn't feel right not telling you anymore."

It changes everything about that day, the crash. I've been picturing him, with the windows down, radio blaring, oblivious that he was running late. I've been picturing him playing drums on the steering wheel and just not paying quite enough attention. I've been picturing a car swerving, causing him to swerve. I've been imagining him having a last thought about me—about loving me—before it ended. But none of that is real.

He'd been on his way to break up with me. Was he feeling dread? Relief? Nausea? All of the above? Was he looking forward to getting it over with and being, what, free?

Like I feel now?

I'm still wearing both necklaces. I take the initial one off and hold it out to her. "You can keep this. It's an *N* anyway, so you're all set."

"Why, so I can pretend he gave it to me?"

"What are you talking about?" How would she possibly know?
~~~

"He wouldn't have bought it for you when he knew he was going to break up with you. I know you bought it for yourself."

"Oh, so what if I did?"

~~~

I go to our spot. Not that there's any reason to think of it that way, not really. But I'm pulled there, as if by a tide.

Of course I want him to be there. For all sorts of reasons. So I can apologize? So I can confront him about how he was talking to Ray like it's no big deal? So I can tell him about Paul.

Of course he isn't there.

Why would he be?

I don't go anywhere near the edges of the ship because my feet are drunks. The wind is a steady fan set to medium-high. My sweater blows open and shut. I find a chair in the center of the deck as close to the indoors as I can. And because I refuse to look at the water, I choose sky.

I choose moon and stars and clouds.

I choose big dippers and little dippers.

I close my eyes and I see 27°58'39.108" N, 82°49'37.505" W behind my lids.

Home seems so very far away now, like a dream within a dream. I've already forgotten what it's like to get up and shower and eat and go to school, and for a second I have to think hard about my locker combination. There's still a photo of me and Paul in there, stuck to the back of the door with putty. In it, we're on the beach—our beach—his arm thrown heavily around my shoulders.

Michael comes through the glass doors near me and stops for a second as we lock eyes. I don't know how I can tell them apart at
~~~

this point—maybe because I haven't seen Ray up close in days—but I can. I regret ever doubting him.

He sits down next to me. "You okay?"

I nod even though it's not entirely true. *Am* I okay? Where to start?

"I saw you and your friends just now. It looked . . . tense."

"I saw you today, too," I say. "I saw you *together*."

"You did?" His head tilts in surprise. "Where?"

"On the beach. You were talking like nothing was wrong—"

"It wasn't like that," he interrupts. "At all."

"What were you doing together?"

"I heard him in his cabin this morning and followed him to the island and confronted him."

"Where has he been this whole time?"

"He was everywhere. Nowhere. I don't know. He says he just got very good at hiding from me and our parents. But he also . . ."

"Also what?"

"He saw us together, I guess? You and me? And, well, he's messing with my head. He was talking about how easy it would be for him to find you and pretend to be me and . . . like, hook up with you."

"That's messed up."

"*He's* messed up. That's what I've been trying to tell you. You didn't see him today, did you? He didn't . . . try anything?"

"No."

"Good." He stretches his legs out on the lounger, accepting that we're going to be a while. "What happened? With your friend?"

It still feels unreal. Saying it will make it more real. I hesitate, but then I let it out. "Turns out my boyfriend was on his way to break up with me when he crashed his car. They just told me."

He lays his head back in his chair, looking up at the sky. "That's a lot to take in."

"Yes, it is." I nod.

"I'm really sorry."

"*And* he was dumping me for one of my best friends."

"One of the friends who's here?"

"Yes."

"Ugh."

We're quiet. The locker combination is 10-25-38. When I next open it up, I'll take down that photo without even looking at it. Truth is I never liked it that much anyway; it's just one of the few actual prints of any photos of us together that I have. I never liked the way I seemed to be collapsing under the weight of his arm.

Michael reaches out and gently squeezes my hand. I swing my legs down to face him, and right then, the wind catches his shirt and blows it off to the side and I get a glimpse of ink on his collarbone, the beginning swirl of the *A* in Amelia. My eyes dart to his wrist—no string bracelet.

The ship rises and falls—or maybe it's just my heart.

I don't know anything.

I'm so sick of people lying.

"I have to go," I say.

"But—" He grabs me, sees me looking at his wrist. "It fell off in the—"

"Let go of me!" I scream, and he does.

I run.

~~~

INT. SUBURBAN BASEMENT -- NIGHT

A shy-looking teenage girl--this is NATALIE--is sitting on a couch and not looking that well. There is a red plastic keg cup in her hand. She puts it down and gets up and stumbles as she walks to a sliding glass door, opens it.

EXT. SUBURBAN BACKYARD -- NIGHT

A dimly lit pool. A covered gas grill. Some bikes strewn on a lawn. She leans against the house, unsteady.

A teenage boy, let's call him ZACK, steps outside with her, walks over, reaches to brush her hair out of her face, leans into her, pushes her up against the wall, and starts to kiss her, then his hand goes up her skirt. He stops kissing but is rhythmically pressing against her. She stiffens and pushes, but it's no use. He's overpowering her.

ZACK

Just relax.
~~~

Another boy--this is MATT--steps out into the yard.

MATT

Everything okay out here?

Zack groans. Natalie walks past Zack and past Matt.

INT. SUBURBAN BASEMENT -- NIGHT

Natalie walks through, head down.

INT. STAIRCASE -- NIGHT

Up she goes.

INT. SUBURBAN FOYER -- NIGHT

She goes out the front door--

EXT. SUBURBAN FRONT PORCH -- NIGHT

--and throws up in the bushes.

~~~

I gasp at gunfire.

No, it's fireworks.
~~~

I'm winded from running, but I think I've put enough distance between us, so I slow to a walk by the shuffleboard courts.

I picture the girls, all gathered on the top deck, watching the sky light up. I can see their faces lit with colors in my mind's eye.

Nora's probably thinking about Paul, about some special moment they shared.

Lexi's probably thinking about Jason and how she'll just not mention Nate at all when she tells him about the cruise because it'd be too hard to explain.

Charlotte; maybe thinking about how different she feels this week, how free.

They're all hopefully maybe a little bit worried about me and what Nora's news will do to me. Maybe they're not even watching the fireworks; maybe they're looking for me.

I think again about the sea below us, whether any creatures down there hear the booms and see flickers of color on the surface of the water. Do they watch with fascination, or do they bury their heads in the sand and worry that maybe the world is ending?

I walk just to walk—the farther the better. I cut through empty dining halls where lights glint off empty metal trays. I drift past the windows of crowded shops. I disappear into a movie theater—usually a favorite place to be—but they're doing a marathon of episodes of an old show called *The Love Boat*, and it's too cheery and dated to bear.

I walk out.

Back on deck, I want to sit, but all the chairs are stacked for the night.

I pass another kid doing the detective stories in the digital paintings. She's trying to solve the mystery of the stolen stars. I want to be that young again, that innocent.

"Natalie!"

He's there. He's chasing me?

But which one is it?

"Don't even talk to me!" I shout.

An elevator opens, and I rush in and hit the door close button frantically.

I get off at a random floor and circle the halls. I want to scream, but something has snatched my voice.

So I just run—and people are staring—and I end up out on a windy deck and have to make sure to stay away from the railings because I don't trust myself not to stumble.

I see lifeboats strapped to the ship above my head and know there are some below me, too. I could carefully climb over a rail and stow away until the coast is clear?

No, that would be insane.

What if I slipped and . . . ?

"Natalie!" His voice again. "I just want to talk!"

The ship is too big, too small; too empty, too crowded.

How could I have been wrong . . . again?

I pass a massive towel cabinet. I could climb in and curl up small among thick white towels.

I want to call Mr. Cassidy and ask him if maybe this is the dark night of my soul.

Or was it the day Paul died?

Or that night at Nora's?

Maybe it's still coming. But when?

A year from now? Or twenty? Tomorrow?

When I'm in it, will I know?

"Natalie! Where are you?" he calls out.

Where do you hide when there's nowhere to go?

~~~

I pound on my parents' door; my mother opens it, half-asleep; reads something in my face.

"Natalie? What is it?"

I let out a sob and she pulls me into a hug and all I can think to say is, "I want to go home."
~~~

★THE STARLITE STARGAZER★

Pisces Day 6!

Bonus! FUN DAY AT SEA

Highlights:

7:00 a.m. — Yoga with Jan
8:00–10:00 a.m. — Omelet Station on the Boardwalk
9:00 a.m.–12 noon — Talent Show Sign-Up at Guest Services
11:00 a.m. — Family Karaoke in the Lunar Lounge
Your professional cruise photographs available for purchase all day, Atrium balcony

Matinee movie: *Seeing Stars* (documentary)

2:00–4:00 p.m. — Acoustic Afternoon on the Aquarius Deck with Mike Maddox
4:00 p.m. — Painting Party—Supernova Teen Lounge
8:00 p.m. — "You're the Stars!" Talent Show! Passengers show off their mad skills: everything from juggling to singing and dancing to hypnosis demonstrations and more. Lunar Lounge
8:00 p.m. — Ping-Pong Tournament—Supernova Teen Lounge
8:00 p.m. and 10:00 p.m. — Stars of the Sea—modern dance extravaganza. NOT TO BE MISSED!

I wake up early feeling different, reset.

The ship is gray everywhere, mirroring the sky—the whole morning like an old movie. I get up off the sofa in my parents' cabin and sneak back into ours and study Nora for a moment; her two-tone hair; her sculptor's nose.

A voice inside me says *it's not her fault.*

Not her fault that she liked him.

I head out, and up, and I cut across the quiet Boardwalk.

The ship is barely awake; there's a man up there on one of the interior balconies and I'm tempted to wave.

Back through another set of doors, I find the Internet café.

I snuck into my house that night, undetected, and crawled under the covers. I had this small sort of sculpture/doll of a girl dancing with a long ribbon that hung over my bed. I'd been talking about getting rid of it, and my mother always said something like, "Oh, don't. It's so pretty, and you've had it forever." I just thought I'd outgrown it. I reached up and tapped it so that it started to spin, and I cried because I wanted so badly to be younger again and more innocent, the kind of girl who'd look at that doll and ribbon and have it spark happy thoughts and daydreams, not doom.

I slept it off and woke up in the morning and pretended I'd just come home. And that everything was fine even though I felt as though someone were wringing my insides like a dishrag.

I'd read the stories about girls who'd been seriously molested for real and raped and Sharpied with obscene things. I'd heard of girls whose lives had been destroyed by photos of stuff they'd done and tweets that got retweeted to infinity. I spent the whole day wondering if he was going to say something bad about me in school, or worse on social media. I wanted to tell someone, but who was there to tell?

I went to the beach. My beach. So in a way, maybe I told the ocean. And I told myself I wouldn't let it change me or define me. I told myself I wouldn't feel shame, even as I felt it.

"Oh my god," Nora said to me that afternoon. "You made out with Todd?"

"Where'd you hear that?"

"My brother said he saw you."

"What else did he say?"

"Nothing," she said. "Why?"

"No reason," I said.

"But it doesn't sound like Todd's, you know, interested, if you're wondering."

"Oh," I said. "Good. Me neither."

I started being really good at finding reasons to not go over to Nora's house. I couldn't handle the idea of looking her brother in the eye. Our school was big enough that I didn't see Todd for weeks, and when I did, I wasn't even sure he remembered who I was. It was better that way.

All in all, I'd gotten off easy.

I resolved to never be that dumb again.

Only when Paul came along could I finally let my guard down. He was so sweet, so cautious, so funny, so like me, it was obvious he was the guy for me. Except that maybe comfort is not the whole of love. Except that maybe I'd never really let him in at all. Didn't want him there, or anyone. Not yet.

~~~

I google “Hitchcock TV show cruise.”

Because maybe it will somehow help me figure out the *why*.

It’s the first hit:

“Alfred Hitchcock Presents” Dip in the Pool (TV Episode 1958) - IMDb

He’d called it that, a dip in the pool, when he suggested the hot tub.

What an arrogant, manipulative jerk.

I’m too impatient to watch the episode, so I read a summary. A passenger on a cruise ship wants to slow down the boat in order to win a bet about how many miles it will travel in a certain number of hours. He figures they will have to stop to rescue him. He chooses a woman he finds on one of the decks to witness his jump into the sea—“Hearing good. Eyesight adequate. You’re it, lady,” he thinks—expecting her to report it. But the woman he picks is mentally ill. She doesn’t say a word to anyone, except to the camera at the end of the episode. She says, after he jumps, “Such a nice man. He waved to me.”

It doesn’t explain anything and certainly not how he could be so cruel to his parents, how he could justify terrorizing a whole ship.

I click away to Instagram and find Nora’s feed, because the Paul thing is still bugging me. I scroll back to a photo of her and Paul I remember her posting. It doesn’t take long to find it; she hasn’t posted much lately.

I hadn’t thought anything of it at the time. Now I see it all differently.

I see their physical ease with each other. I see light in their eyes.

Did they cheat? Go behind my back in some real, physical way?
~~~

It doesn't matter.

I don't love Elvis Moriello.

I wasn't madly in love with Paul. Not anymore, not really, if I ever was.

~~~

I google Michael Haines, but nothing looks right. I just want to know what kind of tracks his life might have left on the Internet. Because of course he didn't just spring to life here, on the boat.

I add "Florida," but still nothing pops out.

I add "Ray," then I add "Amelia," and I click to refresh and feel like I've just gone overboard, too, and bet my whole life on a game of chance.

~~~

"They just started dying": anger lingers over teens who died after . . .

Florida Therapist Settles with Parents of Teens Who Died after Hypnosis . . .

Civil court okays settlement over therapist who hypnotized students with deadly results . . .

Florida Doctor Lied about Hypnotizing Patients Who . . .

Cozy B and B offers luxury accommodations in historic district . . .

~~~
~~~

My brain's batteries are dying; it's malfunctioning, grinding to a halt while spewing out nonsense blips and bleeps. It gets stuck on the word "what" as I frantically click and scan articles.

A local therapist hypnotized teenage patients who were stressed out about tests or sports . . .

What?

He had been reprimanded by at least one family and warned that hypnosis was not a sanctioned treatment . . .

What?

They would report him to a medical board.

But he just kept doing it . . .

Then kids started dying—taking their own lives.

And the one thing they had in common was that they'd had sessions with him.

What?

There was talk of a civil trial, but with no scientific proof that hypnosis is real or can be used to incite self-harm, the odds of a guilty verdict were not good.

The details of the size of the settlements were not made public.

It must be some kind of urban legend or a new Netflix show with an elaborate publicity campaign.

I look it up on Snopes, but it's not there.

The sources are legit. NPR legit.

They all point out how bizarre the story is.

And a part of it feels vaguely familiar? Someone maybe mentioned it in passing once at school?

But I still don't see the connection to Michael and Ray until—

~~~
~~~

A fifth victim, Amelia Haines, drowned in her family's swimming pool after a session with the same therapist. First responders said she was found with a glass floating beside her, so alcohol was suspected as a factor, but during an autopsy her blood alcohol tested at zero. She was believed to be a strong swimmer.

~~~

She's their sister. That's her deal.

Two boys.

Two brothers.

Two tattoos.

~~~

I head out, wishing for a way off the boat, some kind of magical portal to land or a bridge built on the backs of sea creatures who'd surface for me if I tapped out an SOS on the sea. I scan the water for an island I might swim to, and for a second I think I actually see one, but of course not, no.

It doesn't make sense.

At least not to me, not yet.

Their sister died.

Because of hypnosis?

I turn it all around in my head, study the revelation like an object. First, from this side, then from that.

"He didn't make you do anything you didn't want to do, did he?"

"You didn't see him talking to anyone else, did you?"

"There is no floating glass, miss."

~~~
~~~

I pound on Michael's door. So loudly that a woman across the hall comes to answer her door and sun pours out into the hall.

"Sorry," I say, while looking straight past her at the blinding sea through her balcony doors.

Michael's voice comes from behind me. "Sorry, Mom," he says. "She's looking for me."

She lets her door close.

My heart is a sinking anchor when I turn to him. "Why didn't you tell me about your sister?"

He's sinking with me. "Because I didn't want you to look at me the way you're looking at me now."

"Which is how?"

"Like I'm crazy or damaged. Like I'm someone you want to run from like you did last night."

He's shirtless; the tattoo is right there. But I know without question that it's Michael. The way I did last night before doubting myself. "You both have tattoos," I say.

He nods.

"I don't understand, though. All the questions about Ray." A theory forms, like the crest of a wave. "Is *he* hypnotizing people?"

Michael nods again and lets me in. "I think so, yes. Or he's making it seem like he is. Like he probably didn't even take that guy's wallet, just made the guy say that. And the floating glass thing; he must have talked to her. I'm still trying to piece it all together myself. I guess you got on the Internet?"

I nod and say, "I thought *my* life was crazy."

He is standing, looking out the sliding doors. "Yeah, sorry, I think I take the cake."

"*Why* is he doing all this?"

“He just hasn’t been able to accept it, you know, when the guy walked. He’s mad that my parents took the settlement and furious they wanted to go on a cruise, considering how she died. Also, he feels responsible.”

“Why would he feel responsible?”

“We were on a trip once. Vegas. Bunch of years ago now. And there was a hypnosis show at the hotel and he begged my parents to take us all, and then he got really interested in hypnosis and tried it sometimes. Like with Amelia. For fun. Then last year, he started doing this thing at parties. Like one time he hypnotized people at a party and got them to take their shirts off. It was all funny stuff, and everyone thought it was hilarious. But everyone also thought, like I did, that it was just people playing along. It wasn’t real. But I don’t know. He felt like maybe he normalized it. For Amelia. Like she went along with it with the doctor because she thought it wasn’t a big deal, couldn’t hurt her.”

He shakes his head. “My poor mother honestly thought he *made* somebody jump. I actually believed for a minute, too. But now I think he just convinced someone to say that someone had jumped. He’s officially out of control.”

“He threw an inflatable doll overboard.”

“*What*?”

“He made a joke about having an inflatable girlfriend. Everyone says the person who went overboard was blond and naked.” I don’t mention my note or the reply note that confirms it.

“I wouldn’t put it past him,” he says. “And now this is happening.” He hands me a copy of the *Stargazer* and points.

Passengers show off their mad skills: everything from juggling to singing and dancing to hypnosis demonstrations and more.

"What would be the point?" I ask.

"I honestly don't know. But I have to try to stop him."

"Do you even *believe* in hypnosis?"

"I didn't think so before all this. But now it's hard for me *not* to believe."

"Because if you didn't believe, that would mean that your sister—"

"Yeah," he says sadly. "And I mean it's possible . . . but . . ."

"I'll go with you," I say.

"I want to ask you not to," he says. "Except that I really want you there."

"I'm really sorry about your sister," I say, and we fall into a sideways hug and sit with it for a good long while.

~~~

We go down to my parents' cabin and I knock; Michael stays a bit farther down the hall, waits.

My father answers. "The girls just left for breakfast in the Aquarius Room. They were looking for you. Where were you?"

"I woke up early, so I went for a walk," I say. "Anyway, I sort of need a break from the girls, so I'm going to do my own thing today, but don't worry, okay?"

"But, Natalie—" he says.

I look over to Michael, not like there's anything he could even do to help. My mom appears and steps out into the hall.

"This is Michael," I say, and she nods. "Michael, this is my mom."

She meets eyes with me and takes my hand and gives it a squeeze and says, "Have fun."

I squeeze back.
~~~

I go to my cabin and grab a few things: a swimsuit, a cover-up, sunglasses, hat, sunscreen.

"What's this?" Michael picks up the lightbox.

"Was a birthday present," I say, and I think about things I might spell out on it. Things like **ARE WE HAVING FUN YET?**

Or **YOU'RE IT, LADY!**

Or **I FORGIVE YOU, NORA.**

~~~

```
INT. CRUISE SHIP RESTAURANT -- DAY

Three teenage girls--LEXI, NORA, and
CHARLOTTE--are eating breakfast. Lexi wears
sunglasses even though they're inside. She's
buttering a bagel.

            NORA
     How are we going to get through
     the rest of the cruise?

            LEXI
     She'll come around.
```

~~~

I change into my swimsuit and cover-up in a bathroom stall on the Pisces Deck after we eat breakfast. It's early enough that there still aren't a lot of people by the pools. The sun's fire still needs to be stoked.

"Come on," Michael says. "There's like zero line."

"For what?" I say.

"The tube thing," he says.

"Eh," I say. "I'm not really in the mood."

"Well, there's only one way to fix that," he says. "You do it anyway."

"I'm not sure that's a good life strategy." I give him a look. "And anyway, you can't make me do it if I don't want to."

"I wouldn't dare," he says.

He peels off his shirt and walks off across the deck, and in my mind's eye I see myself follow. I see myself stand and let my cover-up fall to the ground. I kick off my flip-flops and put my hair in a ponytail with the tie on my wrist and I call out, "Hey, wait for me." I see him turn and smile. I see him hold a hand out. I see myself taking it.

It could be so easy.

~~~

EXT. CRUISE SHIP -- DAY

A teenage boy--this is MICHAEL--is heading for the waterslide. A teenage girl--this is NATALIE--is watching him go. Looking at him with longing but also with hesitation. She looks up at the tube ride; the people riding it let out happy screams.

NATALIE (*calling out*)
Hey, wait for me.

MICHAEL
That's more like it.
~~~

~~~

He doesn't hold a hand out for me, though. Instead, I take his. It feels almost too bold, so I let go.

There are maybe ten people ahead of us. We wait on the stairs and move up slowly when the line shifts, all without talking. Then it's our turn. We share a tube. Me in front; him behind. His feet tucked around me.

"Well, this is awkward," he says, and I laugh.

Not as awkward as it should be.

We're on a conveyor belt that pulls us out of the loading pool, and the attendant says, "Arms crossed on your chest."

And we're off.

~~~

EXT. CRUISE SHIP -- DAY

A teenage girl--this is NATALIE--and a boy, MICHAEL, are on a tube waterslide. We follow them down a chute, and they fly and scream and whoop. It's a breakneck ride with white foam and sun and the tube is clear so colors whirl by as they pass the main deck, then they are plunged into relative darkness, and then back out into the blazing sun, where they come to a halt. The ride is over.

MICHAEL

Well . . . ?

NATALIE
Let's go again.

~~~

We're back at our chairs after a second run when I say, "You know what's funny?"

"You're not that upset about your boyfriend and your friend?"

"How'd you know?" I ask.

He shrugs.

The fact that he gets it makes me feel less awful about it. "I feel, I don't know . . . released?"

I have not, it turns out, already lost the greatest love of my life before age seventeen. What we had was special, sure, but there's more coming.

"Well, that's good, right?" he says carefully.

"It's weird," I say, wrapping a towel around my waist. "I mean, it was there. Right in front of me, but I didn't see it. I think because this other thing happened that sort of strained things with Nora, I thought it was *that* making things weird and causing us to drift apart. But it wasn't. Or it wasn't *just* that."

"What was the other thing?"

"This thing happened," I say. "At a party at her house. With this guy. I never told her. I never told *anybody*. Instead . . . I don't know. I sort of blamed her?"

"Natalie." He looks at me so seriously that it hurts. He lowers his voice and says, "Were you raped?"

I shake my head. "No," I say. "But I could've been if things had played out differently. Someone interrupted us. Him, I mean. I got
~~~

off easy is how I've been thinking about it. But I realize now that's a bad way to look at it."

"My sister," he says, and I just wait. "I was always telling her to tell me if guys were bothering her, stuff like that, and she was always saying, just stop, nobody's bothering me. But I worried. I think I worried about her more than even my parents did, you know? I feel like they have these blinders on, like they don't realize how bad it is out there."

"I think I had blinders on, too. Or maybe I put them on. After it happened. I just picked this other type of guy entirely, and that made me feel safe. But I was hiding, you know? Hiding in this sort of safe relationship because it was less scary than dealing with the unknown. Paul was a great guy, but I think we were both kind of bored together after a while."

"We're not *all* assholes," Michael says.

"I know," I say.

"It probably doesn't feel that way right now," he says. "I'm sorry I wasn't more up-front at the beginning. It's just all so crazy. It's this thing that happened to me in my life and *I* don't even believe it. How could I expect you to?"

~~~

Mr. Cassidy wouldn't like what happens next at all. Or maybe he'd say, "It's not the *worst* one I've ever seen."

~~~

BEGIN MONTAGE.

One more trip down the tube ride, laughing.

Climbing out at the end and sharing an intense look, his hand landing on her bare hip. A kiss is inevitable but not yet.

Wrapped in a towel, NATALIE is at a soft-serve machine, filling a sugar cone with precision and care. When she's done she turns--too quickly--and her cone rams right into MICHAEL's bare chest. He winces in shock and they laugh. Natalie grabs napkins, starts to help clean him up. Their bodies are so close.

Rock climbing. Natalie is climbing with Michael on belay. She races up the wall and rings the bell. Then she scales the wall back down and faces him, and they unhook from each other.

Riding a carousel; her on a dolphin; him on a sea horse; reaching out hands to close the gap between them.

At the front of the ship. Natalie doesn't want to go too close. But Michael inches forward, arms spread out à la *Titanic*. His heart will go on. Natalie reaches for him, pulls him back from the railings. They are forehead to forehead, touching. He takes her hand, tips his head, they leave together.

```
And enter a small planetarium. Stars sur-
round their first kiss.

END MONTAGE
```

~~~

We're in his stateroom.

I know if I say stop, he'll stop.

Only I don't want to say it.

It's like the damaged version of my self is floating out of me—like a lingering spirit or tortured ghost that finally accepts that it's not welcome here anymore. When it's gone, I'm finally fully there. Exorcized of some of my past hurts. Healed. And for a moment, at least—with our bodies entwined—I'm exactly where I want to be.

~~~

We lie together, just breathing. After a while, I lift my head. "Do you have a picture of her?"

He stands and picks up his phone and wakes it up, and then he scrolls for a bit, taps around, comes back to me.

She has a tiny nose and high cheekbones and an unruly head of wavy blond hair. Her nose is pierced and she has dark eyeliner on that has the effect of making her look even paler than she is. She has a broad smile and a crooked eyetooth and thin lips, and she's wearing a pendant of some kind on a leather choker around her throat. Her eyes are bright and trusting and fearless. I don't know if she's pretty or beautiful or cute or any of those words I hate.

I say, "She looks amazing."

He says, "She was."

Then we're quiet and I want to ask more about her but not if it's painful for him. Finally, he just starts talking. "She had a lot of anxiety problems, you know? Just insecurity kind of stuff that would spiral. Nobody knew why she was so worried about the SAT. I mean, she was so smart. My parents got her therapy because she seemed depressed and then all this . . . And Ray thinks there must have been more to it; more that we'll never know. Like he thinks maybe the doctor did something physical to her? I don't know. And I don't know if we'll *ever* know. I'm coming to peace with that. My brother, not so much.

"All I really want is to find a way to remember her, to honor her, but separate from everything that happened. It's hard. She made that bracelet for me, you know? She'd just sit in front of the TV and make them, and when I thought I lost it in the water, I seriously thought I was going to lose my shit. Even though it's just a dumb string bracelet."

"Wait," I say. "You still have it?"

"Yeah," he says. "I just can't tie it on again. I mean it's physically impossible to do it alone."

"Where is it?"

He goes to get it and brings it over, and I tie it back on for him. Tight.

~~~

I spot the floating glass girl on the way back to my stateroom to shower and change for dinner. She's reading by the pool. I walk over to her. She deserves to know.
~~~

"Hey," I say.

She says, "Hey."

"I wanted to talk to you. About the other night? The floating glass?"

Her expression darkens. "I'm not crazy or whatever."

"I didn't say you were." I slide into the chair opposite her.

"And I wasn't drunk either." She's wearing a really cool swirly tunic, and even in the middle of all of this I'm tempted to ask her where she got it.

"I didn't think you were," I say. "I have a theory, actually."

Now she looks at me like I'm the crazy one.

"Did you meet a guy beforehand?" I ask. "Tall. Good looking. Super charismatic."

She pauses to think, then nods. "Yeah, actually. He was funny. I haven't seen him since then. Do you think he *drugged* me?"

"I think he hypnotized you."

"For real?" she says, and she looks like she might cry and I wonder if it's because it's not the only time in her life a guy has somehow taken advantage of her and how depressing is that?

"Yeah, it wasn't your fault," I say. "It sounds like he can make people do things."

"Why would he do that? Like that specific thing?"

"His sister drowned. There was a glass in the pool when they found her. It's sort of a long story after that."

"That's messed up," she says.

"What did it look like?" I ask after a beat, and I've found my own feet again, like I'm grounded again after being afloat.

She looks confused.

"The glass? Like, was it a regular glass or a champagne flute? What?"

She sighs. "I don't remember. I only sort of remember a feeling. That it was . . . magical."

~~~

Nora's in the stateroom, and for a second I think about just walking out, not dealing.

"Can we *please* talk?" she says, with some attitude.

I can't find words.

She says, "It wasn't my fault."

And even though I've been thinking the same thing, the fact that she says it actually *makes* me mad at her, even if it's just because she doesn't seem sorry, doesn't feel bad either. Shouldn't one of us?

I say, "You fell in love with *my* boyfriend!"

"It wasn't a decision!" She says, "I'm sorry, okay?"

"You don't sound sorry." I sit on the bed.

"We didn't *do* anything, like, physical, if that makes a difference."

"It doesn't." Or does it? I don't know. I don't want to be having this conversation at all except that I also don't want to be the person I was yesterday who was living in some fantasy. I don't even know why we're having the argument. I wasn't even in love with him! But she didn't know that. How could she when I hadn't either?

"Did you, like, hang out behind my back?" I ask, now curious as to the specifics of how it even happened.

She shrugs a shoulder, opens a drawer, and takes out a hot pink bra. "I mean, only a little. And not in some really calculating and planned way. Just we'd see each other places and talk and it sort of developed from there."

"So, like, who made the first move?" I can't believe I'm asking this, but I guess I want to know and be done.

"Move?"
~~~

"You know what I mean." I can't stop looking at the bra.

She sighs. "One day he asked me why I didn't have a boyfriend. And I said something like, maybe the right person's taken."

"Oh, jeez." I get up and go to look at the balcony doors; anything to get her bra out of my line of sight.

"What? I'm sorry. And he said, well, maybe that will change. And then the next time I saw him he was, like, asking for advice. He wanted to know how I thought you'd take it, if he ended it, and I told him that if he wasn't into you anymore, he had to be honest and it didn't matter how you took it."

"Well," I say. "That much is true."

She says, "I don't know what else you want me to say."

"I just wish you'd told me before now." There's no land as far as the eye can see. We're stuck here.

"If I had been able to think of a way to handle it better, I would have," she says. "But then I also got caught up in my own, you know, loss. And having to hide it. And that was really hard."

"I'm sorry."

"Anyway, not like this is an excuse, but we haven't been that close this year. I mean, something changed. You stopped wanting to come over, and things seemed weird."

Of course she would have sensed the shift. It's time to put it behind us, along with everything else.

I turn to her and say, "Something happened the night we were hanging out with your brother's friends. That guy Todd Hendricks. He followed me outside, and he did something I didn't want him to do. Your brother came out and that was the end of it but then I felt like your brother probably misinterpreted what happened but I didn't know how to explain it and then I couldn't stand the idea of seeing them—Todd *or* your brother—at your house so I just started making up excuses."

She looks off into the distance for a minute. "Why didn't you tell me?"

"It felt too weird. I never told anyone. Until today. I told Michael."

Her tone changes, softens—maybe with relief that we've changed the subject. "What's going on with all that?"

"I'm not sure," I say.

"And what about the other one?"

"No idea," I say. "There have been some . . . revelations. Since last night."

"Revelations?"

"It's a lot. I'll tell you all together later, okay?"

"We're doing this painting party thing in like a half hour. You want to come?"

~~~

Blank canvases on stands are perched in front of high stools. There are sets of paints and brushes in plastic-wrapped kits on each stool. The girls have saved a spot for me between Nora and Lexi. They're in the middle of an animated conversation so only nod hi. And I think about turning around and leaving, because that's what I do, except for once I sort of feel like staying. It's a safe place to be for a little while before the talent show. The feeling of dread of actually, finally seeing Ray in the flesh is growing inside me, pulsing like some in-utero alien.

"What about this?" Lexi says. "We show two teens—one of us, one of the guys—and they meet in the teen lounge or something and there's all this chemistry. Like they start dancing together
~~~

without even speaking. And then the song's over and she says, "I have a boyfriend." And he says, "Me, too."

"Wait, he's gay?" Charlotte says.

"Yeah. I mean, that's what's cool about it. It's unclear. It's intriguing. Open to interpretation." She holds up a finger. "No, wait. This is even better. We flip it. Have him say I have a girlfriend and she says me, too. It's even more surprising that way. Right?"

"I like it," I say.

"We can shoot it after this ridiculous gathering," she says, turning to me.

"What are we painting?" I ask.

Nora points to the front of the room, where a completed painting sits on a stand facing us. It's a tropical beach scene, with four Adirondack chairs with their backs to us, a few palm trees.

"It's like they picked it just for us," Lexi says.

"The blue chair is mine," Charlotte says.

"I'll take the peachy one," Lexi says.

"Nat?" Nora says.

There's a lime-green chair and a yellow one. "Green," I say.

"Perfect," Nora says.

Charlotte's Shaun comes in, smiles when he spots her.

"I dared him to come," she says. "He's going to be so bad at this."

The teacher guides us through the painting, and it turns out that Shaun is not as bad at painting a tropical beach scene as Charlotte thought he would be.

"Never underestimate," he says when he reveals his painting, which is near perfect.

Charlotte nods slowly. "I'm impressed."

~~~

Dinner is back in the Top O' the Mast, and it's like I'm a different person since I was last there. We're at the same table we were at four days ago, so we're next to the same fish tank. I can't be sure, but I think there's a fish missing—a sliver of silver that had some blue on its tail; I wonder whether any of the other fish notice that the head count is off.

We chat about everything and nothing—Lexi talks herself out of her two-line movie idea; my father tells an origin story about the word "posh"—"port out, shore home" cabins were considered best; my mother tells a story about a horrible sunburn my father got on their honeymoon. I want to tell them all what I've learned about Ray and Michael and Amelia except not really. Not yet.

The girls think the talent show sounds fun but then luckily decide that the Ping-Pong tournament sounds more fun, so we all head there.

I have a plan.

~~~

INT. TEEN LOUNGE -- NIGHT

A group of teens are gathered around a Ping-Pong table. A girl and a boy--NATE and LEXI--are playing. The competition is tense. Lexi serves. Nate misses. Lexi readies her next serve with a flirtatious smile.

Nearby, another girl--this is NATALIE--turns to the girl--CHARLOTTE--beside her.

NATALIE

I'm just popping out for the talent show.

Charlotte gives her a meaningful, skeptical look.

NATALIE (CONT'D)

I'll explain everything later.

~~~

There's already a sizable crowd in the Lunar Lounge when Michael and I enter. We take seats at the back.

The host is the same crew member who hosted the movie-theme-song game on our first night. He says, "All our performers have been vetted for quality. Just kidding. But they did read the daily newsletter and knew you had to sign up yesterday if you wanted to be a part of this today."

There's still no sign of Ray when it starts.

First on stage is a six-year-old girl named Lucy who sings an amazing jazz song that I don't know but which I think the host said was Nina Simone's. When she's done, the crowd goes wild. Michael and I exchange impressed looks. It's going to be hard to top.

An older woman in a tight dress does a Bollywood dancing sort of number that's pretty cool.

Still no Ray.

The host wheels out a cart full of glasses and a guy gets up and plays a song on them with his fingers on their rims. It's the "Hallelujah" chorus. Also impressive.
~~~

There are a few more singers—a girl sings "Part of Your World" and the whale moms groan—then a guy plays a harmonica, then two sisters do a capable dance routine, then a guy plays piano—that ragtime song the ice cream truck at home plays.

Still no sign of him.

"And for our final act," the host says, "we have a passenger who is going to dazzle us with some of his hypnosis skills. I'll call him up in a second, but we're going to need a few volunteers for this one. Anybody? Anybody? I have five chairs up here, and we're going to need to fill them."

A voice from behind us: "I prefer to choose my own victims."

It's Ray.

"I mean, volunteers."

Michael gets up and blocks Ray's path. "You have to stop."

Ray tilts his head, an uncomprehending robot. "Stop what?"

"I must have had too much to drink at dinner," the host says. "I'm seeing double."

A few people laugh. Ray pushes past Michael and sees me.

I can't believe he showed up.

He can't believe I showed up.

"Okay," he says as he steps up onto the stage. "Let's get this party started. Show of hands for willing volunteers."

I raise mine.

"Natalie, no," Michael says.

"Don't worry," I say. "It'll be fine."

But Ray doesn't call on me. He picks a few other people, but then I'm the only one with my hand still in the air. "Fine," he says. "Natalie."

"Wait," the host says. "You two know each other. Is that like against the rules?"

"Rules, schmules," Ray says, and some people laugh.

"And the rest of you are . . ."

He goes down the row of chairs with the mic and people say their names, "Joe. Lisa. Frank. Angela."

"Nice to meet you all," he says. "Now I want you to concentrate on one thing. I want you to concentrate only on the sound of my voice. Just the sound of my voice. I'm going to say the word "bananas" in a few minutes and when I do, you are all going to fall into a deep sleep, and when I say that same word again, you will wake up in an altered state and will listen only to me."

I don't know whether I believe in hypnosis or not.

I don't think I do, but I'm not sure.

This is the only way to find out.

Ray says, "And here we go. Again, just the sound of my voice, nothing else, no interruptions. You're very relaxed, very focused, the time is now, the time is yours, and bananas."

~~~

There's this thing we learned about in driver's ed called highway hypnosis. It's something that happens to long-distance truck drivers. Their body switches into this mode where they're driving but they don't even realize they're consciously doing it. It's like they get to their destination and wake up there.

I feel truly awake for the first time in my life *while pretending to be hypnotized.*

I hear every word; every joke; every silly thing the other people
~~~

on stage are made to do. I hear every cough. Every laugh. The clank of glasses on tables. The sound of shifting chairs. The underlying hum of the boat.

Ray goes easy on me. He gives me a simple direction, to fall asleep on the person beside me. I lean into the man next to me, wanting to see what Ray will have me do next, wanting to figure out why he is even doing this, why he needs this, what he hopes to prove or find. He moves on. Leaves me there, completely in control without his knowing it.

I think about speaking up, blowing up his game. But all the other volunteers are going along with it, doing increasingly nutty things. Are they actually hypnotized? Will I somehow jeopardize them if I speak up?

I choose silence.

I feel like everything that came before all of this was stuff I let happen but didn't choose.

But you can't go through life in a daze, it turns out.

You need to kick and claw and push and pull and scream.

You need to stand up for what's right—or even just for yourself.

You need to be wide awake.

You need to be exactly where you are whenever you are because blink and you'll miss it.

Anything else is wasting time, wasting words, wasting kisses and turns around the sun.

Anything else is bananas.

~~~

The people beside me look dazed, and I guess I do, too. My
~~~

hair is in my face; I push it out of the way and smooth it behind my ears.

Ray is taking a bow, then he says, "And please, a big round of applause for the real stars of the show." He waves his arm in our direction, and the crowd goes wild. I want to bat away the applause; it's too loud, too close.

"What happened?" the guy next to me says to me.

I don't have time to answer.

Ray's heading for the exit.

I look for Michael. I catch sight of him getting up, and following Ray.

I stand and bolt toward the exit. I see Michael way up ahead down the long hallway, and I run as hard as I can after him.

I catch up to him at the entrance to the crowded Atrium. As I catch my breath, I try to find Ray in the crowd.

"Are you okay?" Michael asks.

I nod and continue to scan the crowd.

"Do you see him?" Michael asks.

"No," I say. "Come on," and we continue down the hall.

We pass a small theater he may have ducked into. I step in and scan the crowd for movement. There's a female comic on stage wearing a T-shirt that says **UNLIKABLE FEMALE PROTAGONIST**.

I dated this guy once who liked to have sex in hotels.

Probably we're not supposed to be here.

But he was broke and couldn't afford that, so he put two double beds in his bedroom at his apartment and hung some bad paintings on the walls.

Chuckles.

He's not here.

A bouncer type is heading our way.

So I was fine with it, but then one night he hands me a bucket and asks me to go down the hall and get some ice.

More chuckles.

We need to leave, but now I want to hear the punch line.

So I dumped him . . .

"Can I see some ID?"

. . . and when I left I stole some towels and shampoo.

~~~

Back out in the corridor, there is no obvious choice for where to go. We end up in the Atrium. I scan the crowd, but he's not there.

Then I see the glass elevator spring into action and I see Ray in it, going up and up and looking down at me and his brother, and he gives me a tiny wave—a flick of the wrist, really—before I say, "Look. There." I point. "He's in the elevator."

Michael looks up just at the exact point where the glass elevator disappears into the belly of the ship.

We've lost him.

"Are you okay?" Michael asks, turning to me.

"I heard everything," I say. "I'm fine. I wasn't hypnotized. I was pretending."

"Anyway, at least it was just party-trick nonsense," he says. "I don't think he's actually out to harm anyone."

We head back down the long corridor.

The room where the talent show had been is now empty; dimly lit. "Come in here," he says.
~~~

I say, "Why?"

"Just bear with me," he says, and he sits down at the piano and indicates the bench, so I sit next to him. He raises his hands so they hover above the keys, their bones somehow newly prominent, and he starts to play. It's classical, lovely. I've never heard it before.

After he finishes, I say, "You should have signed up."

"Not my kind of thing," he says.

And the silence of the room feels different. He's shown me this secret part of him, trusted me with it.

"What's the piece?" I ask, and when he goes to answer, I say, "You know what? Never mind. I like not knowing."

"Why?"

"I don't know. What if I went to listen to it and didn't like it as much as I liked it just now?"

I take his hand and lead him out of the room and head for his cabin. The bones in his hand feel warm and alive as we wind our way down corridors and under the anchor in the Atrium and up the elevators to his floor.

A steward is in the hall by his stateroom and says, "Did you get a replacement card, sir?"

Michael stops abruptly. "Excuse me?"

"For your lost card, sir."

"I didn't lose my card. It must have been my brother." Michael goes to open his stateroom door.

"You are Mister Ray, yes?"

"No, I'm Michael."

"But . . . he said he was you, sir." The steward looks nervous now. "I was working in your stateroom earlier. I let him in."

~~~
~~~

Nothing seems out of order. Michael tells the steward so and says not to worry.

"What could he have wanted in here?" I ask when we're alone.

"I have no idea," Michael says. "But he must have known I'd fall for his talent show trap, so he knew I wouldn't be here."

We go inch by inch, looking for anything that might be some kind of clue to what he's up to. I peek into the closet and see the safe. "Is there anything in the safe?"

"My wallet and passport." Michael comes over and punches in four numbers.

His wallet is there but no passport; he takes the wallet out and looks through it. "He took my license, too."

"Why would he . . . ?"

"I have no photo ID. It means I can't get off the ship in Key West."

His brother's words from days ago pop up like a newly sprung buoy. "He said he had business to attend to in Key West."

"What?"

"That first night. What does it mean?"

"Well," he says. "I don't know. But remember I said he was really resistant to the cruise idea?"

"Yes."

"My parents dragged their heels booking it because he was being difficult, but when they decided that they really wanted us to go somewhere, the itineraries for what was available changed. And he wasn't that opposed anymore. The first cruise they were looking at didn't go to Key West at all."

"What's so special about Key West?"

"I don't know. But even if we figure it out it doesn't matter if I can't get off the boat," he says. "I need to talk to my parents. Maybe they brought photocopies or something? I have no idea. I have to go to guest services, I guess."

"You really have no idea what he's up to?" I say, feeling like he wants to be rid of me.

"I really have no idea what he's up to," he says as he opens the door. "But I need to find my parents."

"You'll let me know as soon as you find out anything?"

"Of course."

"Hey," I say, in the hall. "Our phones will work once we're in port."

We exchange numbers, and that small thing feels at least a little bit normal.

~~~

The girls are up; they're waiting for me.

Our four paintings are perched up against the wall on top of the long cabinet. It's not hard to tell whose is whose. Like Shaun's, Charlotte's came out near perfect; an exact replica of the instructor's. Lexi's is more loosey-goosey—a good impression of someone who wants to stay in the lines but can't. And Nora's is somehow brighter, somehow sunnier. Mine is proficient but somehow muted.

"Tell us everything," Lexi says.

"Promise me you won't look at me like I'm crazy."

"Okay," Lexi says. "Promise."

When I'm done telling them about Amelia and the other students who died, about the doctor, about Ray's guilt and attempt to make his parents miserable, Charlotte says, "That is messed up."

"I think I remember hearing about that at school," Nora says, with a strange tone. "I mean, someone said something? I don't know."

"I had that feeling, too," I say.
~~~

Lexi says, "But hypnosis *isn't* real."

"I don't know," I say. "It didn't work for me, but maybe it does for some people?"

"He needs professional help," Lexi says. "I mean, they both do. Ray *and* the doctor."

"Yes," I say. "That's true."

"So that's it, then," Lexi says. "You got your answers."

"Well . . . ?" I say.

"What?" she asks.

"He told me he had business to attend to in Key West. And he stole Michael's IDs, so now Michael can't get off there."

"Why would he do that?" Charlotte asks with genuine curiosity.

~~~

We get ready for bed; there's a fluid rhythm to it by now; the Greek chorus perfectly in sync.

In the dim light of the room I look at the people waving goodbye to the boat in the illustration on the wall. I close my eyes and try to picture them turning and being just normal happy people; I want very badly to create an antidote to my dream.

But every time, no matter how hard I try to imagine a better scene, a better dream, the black eyes are still there, and now they belong to skeletons.

~~~

Natalie. Natalie.

A hand on my shoulder.

"We have to talk."

I must be dreaming but no. Awake.

I look up at Nora, then at the clock: 3:07 a.m. I whisper, "What's wrong?"

"Follow me." She puts my hoodie beside me and slips out onto the balcony. I peel out of bed, pull on my hoodie, and follow.

She sits in one of the two chairs with her legs tucked up under her oversized sleep T-shirt. "I talked to him the other day on the island. Ray. On the island."

"You said you saw him, not that you talked to him."

"I didn't want you to know. But I was curious about this guy you're so crazy for, so I talked to him."

"About what?"

"I asked him why he blew you off."

"Ugh. Why did you do that?"

"I wanted to know what his deal was."

"What did he say? How did you know which one it even was?"

"He told me which one. And he said he felt like he was going to tell you things he shouldn't tell you if he saw you again, so he left."

"I don't know what that means or how to feel about it."

"He said he thought he would get too close or something. And he didn't want you to know what he was doing."

"What is he doing?"

"I don't know!"

"Did he make you do anything weird?"

"No," she says. "But he did this thing where he cupped his hand to his ear and he said, 'Do you hear that?' And I said, 'Hear what?' And he said, 'The siren's song.' "

"What does that mean?"

"I thought you might know," she says. "That's why I'm telling you." Then she shivers. "The whole thing gave me the creeps."

"And why are you only telling me this *now*?"

"Well, I wasn't going to tell you at all," she says. "But not telling you stuff hasn't exactly worked out great before. I couldn't sleep."

"We should get back to bed," I say, and she stands.

"I'll be right in," I say.

The sky is pocked with stars, each one a tiny burning wound.

~~~

EXT. CRUISE SHIP BALCONY -- NIGHT

A teenage girl--this is NATALIE--sits alone, staring at the night sky. Her hand goes to her necklace, like she just wants to be sure it's still there.

She stands and steps closer to the railing, cautiously looking over and down. Waves crash against the ship's hull.

She closes her eyes, like she is listening so very hard, and the sound of the waves gets louder and mixes with a piano song and when she opens her eyes, the piano fades and the waves soften and she turns and goes inside.
~~~

★THE STARLITE STARGAZER★

Pisces Day 7!

Port of Call: Key West, Florida

7:00 a.m. — Wake-Up Jazzercise
11:00 a.m.–2:00 p.m. — Mahjong in the Saturn Room
1:00 p.m. — Matinee movie DOUBLE FEATURE: *The Spanish Prisoner* (shot on Key West!) and Ernest Hemingway's *For Whom the Bell Tolls*

3:00–5:00 p.m. — Live music in the Atrium—family friendly!—Judy and the Blooms play kids' classics!

6:00–8:00 p.m. — Pop-Up Key Lime Pie station—Boardwalk
7:00 p.m. — Supernova Foosball tournament
8:00 p.m. and 10:00 p.m. — Magic of the Movies cabaret—The Starlite Theater

I text him but he doesn't text back.

I call but he doesn't pick up.

Then my parents are there and we're all getting off the boat and I'm in a van on my way to Hemingway's house before I can figure out a way to do anything else.

The day feels like a ticking time bomb, like a countdown to disaster.

I listen hard, for some siren's song, but I don't hear a thing.

~~~

Hemingway's house is verandas and wooden shutters. Palm trees and flowering bushes. Grand staircases and high windows.

"I'd rather be at Judy Blume's house," Lexi says as we begin our tour.

"What?" I laugh.

"She lives down here, too. And I mean, just in terms of influence on my life, I'm pretty sure Judy has Ernest beat."

The same may be true for me but still, I like it here.

When we read *The Great Gatsby* last year I felt like maybe I'd been born during the wrong era. Or maybe just born without the right amount of money. I dressed up as a flapper that Halloween—straight black dress and long white pearls, hair in sculpted waves finished with a bedazzled headband, the kind that runs across your forehead—and everyone said it suited me.

The tour guide is droning on. The takeaways are that Hemingway was a manly man and had many wives and mistresses and tragedies and loved fishing and Cuba and adventure. I perk up when he mentions that Hitchcock asked Hemingway to write the screenplay for *Lifeboat*. I spot, inside a glass case next to me, a copy
~~~

of the 1943 telegram that Hemingway sent in reply to the offer, politely declining to take the job.

I take a picture of it for Mr. Cassidy.

~~~

Charlotte and I end up sitting by Hemingway's pool alone when the tour winds down. A few of the house's famous cats are skulking around and could not be less interested in us.

"I can't imagine turning down working with Hitchcock," I say.

"I don't know," she says. "Didn't it come out recently that he was accused of being a sexual predator?"

"Really?"

"I think so," she says, and she gets her phone out. "The actress from *The Birds*?"

She goes to look it up, but I'm just happy watching the cats.

There's a screenwriting book Mr. Cassidy refers to sometimes called *Save the Cat*. The title comes from the idea that when you introduce the hero of a story, he (or she) should do something nice, like save a cat that is about to meet its demise, so that the audience likes him or her. We talked through some examples once, but at the end of the discussion it still felt to me like a sort of dumb device that audiences would see right through.

"Yeah, Tippi Hedren says he ruined her career," Charlotte says.

I say, "That sucks," and I wonder whether Mr. Cassidy knows about that and cares.

She says, "Did you know Hitchcock made a movie called *Lifeboat* about a group of people stuck on a boat together?"

"In fact I did," I say. "Just like us!"
~~~

One of the garden cats finds a spot of interest on the ground and starts digging at it with its front paws, frantically.

"What do you think that's about?" I say.

"Dead body," Charlotte deadpans, as the cat stops, stretches, moves on. "Has to be."

~~~

We head for a bar that the tour guide said Hemingway used to frequent, which seems sort of silly since we can't drink, but my parents are determined so we tag along.

At the bar we order Cokes, and then we find a high table near the windows looking out on the street.

My phone rings. I pick up.

"Finally," I say.

"Hey," he says. "So they won't let me off the boat. Promise me you won't try to find him."

I say, "Does the phrase 'siren's song' mean anything to you?"

"No, why?" His voice sounds small.

Through the window, I see the man with the Mets cap—the one who I guess accused Michael of stealing his wallet.

"Never mind," I say, "I have to go."

"Natalie, promise me you won't—"

I walk out to the sidewalk but somewhere between the table and here I've lost him and I'm not sure I would have had the nerve to ask him about Ray, whether it's possible he was also hypnotized.

Charlotte has followed me out and says, "Who are you talking to?"

"Michael. He says they won't let him off the boat," I say to her.

She scrunches up her face. "That doesn't make sense."

"What do you mean?" I ask.
~~~

"You don't need ID to get *off* the boat. Just a key card, which they replace if you lose it. So he could just walk off. He might not be able to get back *on*, but that's different."

"So he's lying to me?" I say.

"Why would he do that?" she says.

"He's already figured it out," I say.

"Figured what out?" she says, shaking her head.

"Ray said he had business in Key West. He's got something planned."

Nate and Ben and Leo appear out of the crowded street. We tell them about the Hemingway tour and they tell us about their trolley ride and then Ben turns to me and says, "I figured out what we missed in the escape room."

"Yeah? What?" I honestly haven't given it another thought.

"We got too focused on greed," he says. "Or I did anyway. The killer wasn't there to steal the money. It was a *payment* for the killer. He'd been hired to kill Ava. We would have figured it out if we turned the lights off and turned the flashlights on. There was a note written in black-light ink on the front desk with instructions for the killer, who was the owner, by the way. He'd been hired by the ex-husband because Ava had cheated on him. So it was a different popular motive for murder . . . Not greed but . . ."

I watch Ben's mouth about to form the word. Life grinds to slow motion as the reel starts to melt: "Revenge."

~~~

My phone feels weird in my hands, as the boys continue on their way. A trolley rolls past, leaving the muffled voice of a tour guide talking through a megaphone in its wake.
~~~

"I missed something," I say.

"You're not making sense," Charlotte says.

I say, "Nora said she talked to Ray and he asked her if she heard the siren's song."

I open Safari. I put in the twins' names and Amelia's name, and this time I add Key West.

The results are different from last time by a bit, with the listing about a B and B that seemed out of place last time now popping up in the first slot.

Cozy B and B offers luxury accommodations in historic district . . .

I click the link and end up on the B and B's site.

The Siren and Crocodile Inn is a charming old Key West building that has been updated with all modern amenities in a stylish fashion . . .

I tap "About the owners."

Bill and Terri Straus are your proud hosts and will make sure your time in Key West is relaxing and enriching.

I go back to my search and reread one of the main articles about the whole story.

The doctor, William Straus, has moved out of the county. He agreed never to practice again and is rumored to be operating a B and B elsewhere in the state.

~~~

Charlotte won't want to come with me so I don't even ask.

I calmly say, "Let's go back in."

We join our group and I pull Nora aside and say, "I need you to come somewhere with me."
~~~

"Where?" she says.

"I think I know where Ray is going."

"This doesn't seem like a good idea," she says. "And there's barely time. We have to be back on the boat in like an hour . . ."

"I know but . . . *please*."

She gives me this look, and it seems to sum up everything that's been between us—the deceptions, the jealousy, the lies, the hidden resentments—and I say, "I need to see this through. After tomorrow they'll be gone forever and I'll never know what it all meant."

"I don't know, Nat," she says.

"You're the only one who can do this with me." I nod toward the others. "I mean, look."

She follows my gaze; Lexi and Charlotte are chanting, "We must. We must. We must increase our bust."

"Fine," Nora says. "Let's go."

~~~

My phone leads us away from the bars with crowds spilling out onto the street, and, soon, we're on quiet residential streets. The houses are small and adorable, and I'm thinking *who the hell lives here*, which I think pretty much everywhere I go. I wonder if that feeling ever stops, if you're ever in the world enough that you get it: People are not all like you. They live other places and have totally different lives than yours and they're fine. Maybe even better than fine.

Maybe half the reason I'm never happy where I am is that I'm living in the wrong place.

Maybe I *should* go away to college.

I should go to film school, wherever that is.
~~~

Google says it's a ten-minute walk to the B and B, but we can do it faster than that, I know it.

I track us in the app, feeling somehow comforted by the moving arrow on the screen, showing us getting closer to . . . what, exactly?

~~~

INT. AN INN -- DAY

A man is gagged and tied to a chair in a guest room. He's sweaty and bloody. He's been here awhile.

A younger man, RAY, comes into the room, carrying a selection of knives on a tray.

RAY

Now, where were we?

Groans from the gagged man. He pulls at his restraints, tries to move the chair with body bounces.

Ray turns around with a knife in his hand.

RAY

Oh, right, we were talking about my sister.

~~~

The flowers lining the main path look like the heads of tropical birds. A set of sheer ivory drapes dances out an open door on a high veranda. A sign out front, predictably, shows a siren and a crocodile sharing a rocky perch.

The front steps bend and squeak. I stand at the front door, a combination of wood and frosted glass. I put a hand on the heavy metal knob and turn.

Our phones buzz.

We quickly silence them and head in.

Soft music plays—some kind of creole/zydeco—but there is no one at the front desk. Only a cup of coffee that looks abandoned, cold. There's a bell to ring for service but that seems like a bad idea, then Nora does it anyway.

It's louder than it should be, or maybe just seems louder than it is. No one responds.

Nora and I swap a look, and I step toward the open door opposite the entrance. I go through it and into a quiet courtyard garden. There's a small neglected pool with a slightly green tint; multiple dead flies floating.

A mermaid fountain trickles water into a small collecting pool. A few metal bistro tables and chairs sit on an uneven bluestone patio. The air smells of chlorine and gardenias.

"Hello?" I call out.

There's no one there.

"Natalie," Nora whisper-screams. "Come here."

I go back to the lobby, where she stands at the threshold. She points up. A thump from overhead shakes the ceiling fan.

"I'm calling the cops." Nora reaches for her phone.

"Wait," I say. "Not yet."

I head for the stairs. It's a wide curved wooden staircase that takes up half the lobby's air space. I try a few doors on the first floor hall—locked—then see a door open a crack at the end of the hall. The floorboards squeal under my feet.

"Ray?" I say softly. "Are you here? It's me, Natalie."

I peek through the opening in the doorway—a cat *or something* darts across the room. I reach out and start to open the door and it shrieks the whole time.

Grunts from the far side of a large four-poster bed.

"Ray?"

More grunts and another thump.

"Michael?" I try.

I take a deep breath and close my eyes and prepare myself for the worst.

~~~

INT. AN INN -- DAY

An empty lobby; no one at the front desk. In walks a teenage girl--this is NATALIE--and she clearly has something on her mind. She moves as if in slow motion, careful steps.

She climbs a winding staircase and climbs some more, then reaches a top floor, an open door. Curtains blowing from an open veranda door. She steps out, the railing is broken. She crosses
~~~

to it. Looks down. A body floating in the swimming pool below.

A sound behind her. She turns. It's RAY.

NATALIE
I'm sorry about your sister.

RAY
She was a very strong swimmer.

~~~

I step into the room and walk toward the sound, and he says, "Who's there?"

Not Ray. Not Ray's voice.

Not Michael either.

He pulls himself away from the bed and stands and says, "Can I help you?"

"I was looking for my friend." I can't bear being in the same room as him but don't have a choice.

"Sorry." He's holding a wad of foul-smelling paper towels and goes to put them in a plastic bag. "Goddamn cat puked under the bed."

This is the guy.

This is the guy?

I don't know what I'd been expecting. Someone young and charismatic, maybe. Someone handsome that patients would admire. But he's a short, stout, balding man who, by the looks of it, sweats
~~~

a lot. His thick gold wedding ring looks too tight on his hands, and his shorts can't seem to find a waistline.

Nora's hanging back at the door to the room, just waiting.

This is not what we'd been expecting, and I'm not sure whether I'm relieved or disappointed.

"Was Ray just here?"

"Let's talk downstairs," he says, "after I get rid of this."

He heads for the hall and we follow and he disappears into a bathroom and comes out, drying his hands with a paper towel, then he goes down the stairs and settles in at the front desk. "Now who are you looking for? Our guest list is private, so—"

"Ray Haines," I say. "His sister was one of the people you—"

"I had one visitor stop in earlier—nice young man—didn't say anything about a sister. Said he was looking for a place for his parents to stay for their anniversary next year."

Nora and I share our confusion with a look.

"You seriously don't know who he was?" I ask.

"He famous?" he asks.

"No," I say. "It's nothing like that. His sister was one of the people who died. After you hypnotized them."

It's like he's been infected with malware. His voice is full of menace when he says, "I'm going to have to ask you to leave now."

"Why did you do it?" I ask. Because if Ray didn't, I have to.

"I didn't intentionally harm anyone," he says flatly. "Which is more than he can say."

"What does *that* mean?" I say.

"I'm done talking," he says.

Nora is backing away toward the front door. "Nat, he's not here," she says. "We really have to go."

~~~

We run hard. The boat can't leave without us. We can't let that happen.

Our phones light up.

Texts from Lexi and Charlotte.

Where are you guys?

Why aren't you answering?

We'll hold the boat if we have to.

Please don't make us have to!

My body isn't made for this. I'm winded and burning.

When we finally arrive at the port, they're waving their arms, as if we don't know where to go, as if the ship isn't right there.

"Where were you guys?" Lexi asks.

"Everything okay?" Charlotte says to me, more meaningfully.

I'm too winded to talk.

We sanitize and go through security, then stop on a lower deck to catch our breath. When I can, I explain where we were, who we saw.

"I don't understand," Nora says, in conclusion.

I say, "Me neither."

"Why did he go there if he wasn't going to do anything to him?" Lexi asks.

"I don't know," I say. "Maybe he thought he'd do something, then couldn't go through with it?"

Which is more than he can say. What did that mean?

~~~

Back in the cabin, Charlotte wants to shower.

Lexi needs to pee.

That leaves me and Nora alone on the balcony.

"I had this clarinet teacher when I was in middle school," she says. "And he . . . he just was so gross. He'd say stuff like 'stand up and let me see how much you've grown,' and I just didn't know until a lot later how not cool that was. At the time, I just knew it made me feel weird, you know? Anyway, that guy today. I don't know what he did or whatever, but he reminded me of him. The clarinet teacher. My parents never got why I wanted to stop taking lessons because I never told them. I never told anybody."

I nod, wondering whether there was an exact point in time where life got complicated for all of us.

"I'm sorry about what happened at my house," she says. "You know it wasn't your fault, right?"

For a second I might cry but then the boat is making this crazy U-turn and the sun hits us hard and I slide my sunglasses onto my face and feel like I can do anything. I pull Nora into a hug.

"You're not going to like this," I say when I release her.

"I know," she says, and I realize she's crying. "You're going to go talk to him," she says. "The other one."

"Michael." I nod.

Nora sighs away her tears. She says, "I just want things to be normal again. And simple. Fun, even." She half smiles. "I want us to go back and be dumb high school seniors and have a great year and not have any more weirdness between us and not have any insane things happen to us and that's it really. Is that so much to ask?"

"No," I say, squeezing her arms. "It's going to be like that, I promise. It's going to be epic, the rest of this year, seriously. We're going to grab life by the whatever-you-grab-life-by and live large.

For real. We're going to be royals. We're going to be amazing and do things people will talk about for years and no one's going to be able to touch us."

"So don't go," she says, but I can see in her eyes she knows I have to.

~~~

I knock and he opens. His hair is wet, the bracelet on his wrist. His eye is swollen above a purple cheekbone, and he has a fresh cut on his lip.

I say, "What *happened*?" right as he says, "What's wrong?"

He takes my hand, his eyes full of worry.

"Your brother," I say. "He found the doctor."

"*What*?" he says. "Come in, come in. How do you know this? Were you there? Are you hurt?" Looking around, he says, "The place is a mess, come out here." He goes through the open balcony door.

I follow. You can feel how fast the ship is moving already, the wind whipping through its channels.

I say, "I'm fine. I figured it out. The doctor owns a B and B here now. Ray went there."

"And he brought you?" he says. "Sorry, I'm just confused about how—"

"No, when I figured it out I went there."

"Why?"

"To stop him, I guess?"

"Stop him from what?"

"I wasn't sure! I'm still not. I mean he definitely went there, but he didn't even tell the doctor who he was. He was gone by the time I got there."
~~~

He sits down, sighs. "After all this, you still needed to go after him. He's still the one you . . ."

"It's not like that." I step closer to him. "I thought you'd figured it out. I thought you got off the boat and lied to me to protect me. I thought you'd be there."

"I'm sorry I wasn't," he says. "I've been going crazy wondering what was happening. But my parents wouldn't let me get off."

I kiss him, hard, and we grab at each other for a frantic minute and then the mood breaks and something feels off. His parents weren't the ones stopping him from getting off . . . Were they? When I pull away I lean my forehead on his tall chest and look down, avoiding eye contact until I can figure out why I'm hearing alarm bells. On the small low table beside us, I see his key card.

RAYMOND HAINES

I reach down and pick it up for a closer look.

"Ah, crap," he says, then he leans out over the railing and shakes his head and smiles back at me. "Admit it. You've missed me."

~~~

You want to believe that people are good.

You know that there are warlords and murderers and kidnappers and terrorists in the news and in the world. But in the day-to-day of your normal life, you want to believe that you don't have to be on the lookout for evil or malice. You want to believe you'd smell it a mile away if it did exist. You'd be smarter. Wiser. You wouldn't be duped.

You want to believe that if you were in trouble, the stranger who
~~~

stopped to help would call you a cab, send you home, not drag you behind a dumpster and cut you into pieces.

You want to believe that you can go out and embrace the world with open arms and be okay.

You want to believe that no means no.

You want to believe that people will always do the right thing.

Even you.

But you don't know for sure until you're there.

~~~

"Where is he?" My voice is gravel. I have to clear stones of anger away to make room for air. The ship vibrates urgently underfoot.

"*That's* what you want to know?" he says. "Don't you want to know why I went all the way there and didn't, like, kill the guy?"

"Fine. Tell me."

"While it might appear that I didn't do anything, I actually did do something," he says.

"What?" I say. "What did you do?"

"Here's what's going to happen to Bill. Bill is going to go about his business thinking everything is just peachy. He's going to think that whole messy chapter of his life is over and that he's sitting pretty in his cozy little B and B. But then one day—and it might be tomorrow, or it might be a few years from now—he's going to hear my sister's favorite song on the radio. And when he does, he's going to stand up in the middle of whatever he's doing. It won't matter if he's cooking breakfast for some guests or taking a little dip in his pathetic green pool or getting a haircut or shopping at a mall. He's going to stand up and walk out of wherever he is, right into traffic."
~~~

"I don't understand," I say.

"We had a little chat, me and Bill. He won't remember it. And he won't understand either why that seemingly random and just plain silly song about a yellow submarine just compels him to walk right into harm's way. He won't have the time to figure out that it's all because I just gave him a little dose of his own medicine."

"You did that? Got those people on the ship to sing?"

"People are ridiculously easy to manipulate," he says.

"Where's Michael?" I ask, feeling the fuzzy edges of fear.

"I honestly have no idea," he says. "The last time I saw him, he did *this* to me." He makes a circular kind of gesture around his face. His cheekbone has turned an even darker purple. I can taste his blood on my lips, and it makes me want to throw up. I can feel the start of a dry heave in my stomach; some kind of release that has to come one way or another. "I told him what I'd done with his passport and license, and he was not pleased."

He shakes his head at me and says, "I honestly don't understand what you see in him."

And I hear his words like in slow motion along with *Just relax*, and *Everything okay out here?* and *Stand up and let me see how much you've grown*, and I'm so tired of being a girl and being judged and having to navigate this whole new world of desire and fear that I charge at him like I'm the walking dead, with nothing to lose.

I push against his chest with every last bit of anger I have in me, and, on impact, his expression changes from some kind of arrogance to fear. I've caught him off guard and he's so tall and his center of gravity is so high . . .

Oh my god.

He's falling.

Over the railing.

I almost laugh.

He reaches out for me and catches only my necklace, which breaks free but then falls from his grip. The silver bar catches the sun and glints and then seems to swim in the air between us.

Paul's up there, on his cloud-throne, and he covers his mouth and says, "Oh shit!"

Maybe this is what it feels like, to see the floating glass no one else can see.

~~~

Metal warms my palm as I snatch the necklace from the air.

Of course, I bought it for myself. Because yes, it was the beach where I used to hang out with Paul, but before that, it was the place I used to go to alone, when I was feeling low or lost or just not wanting to be wherever else I'd been.

It was the place where I went after Todd, the place where I decided to try not to let someone else's actions define me, the place I returned to each time I felt shame and knew I'd failed.

I'll go back there again when I get home; the sand will feel the same on my toes, but I'll know I'm different now.

I'm still here.

And as Ray falls out of sight, I feel so deeply at peace for once that I barely hear the horrified screams—like dolphins being slaughtered—coming from the deck below.

~~~

EXT. CRUISE SHIP -- BALCONY -- DAY

A teenage girl--this is NATALIE--stands at the balcony rail. The door to the cabin opens and she turns. It's MICHAEL, looking distraught.

MICHAEL

Oh, Natalie. What have you done?

NATALIE

Only the thing you couldn't.

✯NOTES ON DISEMBARKATION✯

ALL PASSENGERS MUST VACATE THE SHIP BY 9 A.M.

Luggage must be left outside staterooms by 10 p.m. tonight in order to be carried off the ship by crew.

Bags not put outside tonight must be carried off by passengers.

Please remember to check all drawers and closets and safes before disembarking!

THANKS FOR SAILING WITH US! AND BE SURE TO BOOK YOUR NEXT STARLITE CRUISE LINE VACATION SOON!

I wake up happy when my phone's alarm goes off. Nora turns over in her bed. Lexi doesn't move. Charlotte is snoring almost imperceptibly, and the combination of the sound, and her soft features, and the delicate tendrils of braids that stretch out on her pillow make her seem just so content.

They're good friends and that means everything. I should have leaned on them more when Todd Hendricks did what he did to me at that party. They would have had my back, and I should have let them.

We would have talked about how hard it is to figure out what you want when you don't even know what the what *is* before you've done it.

Maybe we would have talked about feeling bad for saying no to guys, because what the hell is that even about? Maybe we should have talked about the kinds of guys we knew we should steer clear of. The ones who behave more like boys than men.

In regular life you don't get to see all sides of a person. You don't get to watch them sleep that way my mother says she used to watch me sleep when I was a baby. I think I finally understand that impulse now in a way I never did before. When you watch someone sleep—even if it's your friend who fell in love with your boyfriend, or your friend who probably would have cheated on her boyfriend if she could have, or your friend who struggles quietly, without fuss, with who she is—you see them at their most vulnerable and peaceful self.

This is why we all try so hard—to be smart or pretty or popular or different or the same.

This is why we go to school and get jobs and learn to play instruments and swim with dolphins.

This is why we build ridiculous things like cruise ships in the first place.

It's because we're scared out of our minds.

We're *always* just inches from death and we know it.

~~~

I'm meeting Michael to watch the sunrise.

He's there, on our deck, with a blanket and two cups of hot tea.

I slide under the blanket with him, and we watch the sky turn white then pink then blue. With each shift, it seems to change not at all, then all of a sudden.

I'm not sure what there is left to say, so I don't say anything.

"Well, there's one thing I learned on this cruise for sure," he says, after a while.

"What's that?" I ask.

"Always get the room with the *interior* balcony," he says.

I laugh, even though it's sort of a horrible thing to laugh at.

Ray fell two stories from Michael's balcony before landing on the soft canvas of the Boardwalk carousel. He didn't end up with so much as a scratch—or at least none in addition to the ones Michael already gave him.

While people rushed to assist him, I left the cabin and went back to mine and I didn't say a word about my involvement to anyone and he, apparently, didn't either. Except to Michael, who'd then found me in my cabin.

"What are you going to do about him?" I asked.

"Get him some kind of help," he said. "He finally said he'll do it. He said he gets that now it's time."

"You believe him?" I asked.
~~~

"I have to," he said.

Then I introduced him to all the girls and we all—even my parents—went to the big buffet together since we missed our official dinner sitting and it was a better sort of birthday dinner than the original birthday dinner had been for sure.

Now, he sweeps my hair out from the back of my neck admiringly, kisses me on the head, and says, "I could come visit you, you know? Like soon."

"Maybe," I say, thinking about Paul and how I let it all happen without ever making it happen and thinking that I won't be doing that again.

"It's not that far at all."

"Maybe," I say, not convinced I see us together back in real life, and that seems like one of the most important things in life to be convinced of—whether you want to spend time with a person.

"I should kiss you. I mean, if you want."

"Definitely," I say. Because that is one thing I'm sure of, even if it's just for right this second. "Want."

I close my eyes and the world around me is a circle of soft light that starts to shrink until it's no bigger than the hole a thumbtack makes on a map and then it's gone and I'm somehow on the other side of it.

"What's with the numbers anyway?" He is looking at my necklace.

"Map coordinates."

"Of . . . ?"

"A special place."

He nods and he doesn't ask any more. A seagull lands on

the railing about ten feet from us. Then another. And then another.

"You ever see the Hitchcock movie *The Birds*?" I ask.

"Sure," he says. "A bunch of years ago. Why?"

"Why do you think they did it?"

"Why did the birds attack, you mean?"

"Yeah."

"I don't know."

"Doesn't that seem like a cop-out?"

"Not really." He shifts his position and I have to shift, too. "I mean it's sort of the whole point, right? It's this dark force in nature we'll never understand."

"I guess I like happy endings better." I stand. "I need your help with something before I go."

Then I explain as I get my phone propped up at just the right angle.

"Wait," he says. "You're only going to *pretend* to choke me. Right?"

"Of course."

"Well, for the record, you've got a pretty weird definition of a happy ending."

~~~

```
INT. CRUISE SHIP CABIN -- DAY

A girl--this is NATALIE--is sitting with her
eyes closed on the bed. A boy--this is RAY--
is holding a pendant, waving it in front of
her face.
```
~~~

RAY

You are getting very sleepy.

Natalie's eyes shoot open, and she goes to choke him.

NATALIE

No, I'm not.

~~~

Back in the cabin the girls are looking in closets and drawers, making sure we're not leaving anything behind. We take damp swimsuits down from the line in the shower. We slip our beachy paintings into side pockets of suitcases, though honestly, I'd be happy to just ditch mine and maybe I will when we get home. None of us could get our act together to put bags out last night and when I'm zipping mine closed I find the box the necklace from Nora came in and I grab it and something inside it shakes. I open it and the necklace is back in there.

I take a final look at the art on the wall, of the crowd waving to the ship—the backs of those eye-less faces I dreamed about. It's such a remarkably mediocre piece of art that it feels hard to imagine how it triggered such a vivid nightmare.

"I had a dream the other night that all these people in this drawing turned around and had black holes for eyes," I say.

"Cool," Lexi says as she zips up her suitcase and sets it to standing position. She stayed out late last night, later than the rest of us. With Nate. I've already resolved not to ask her what she did or didn't do.
~~~

“None of you ever ended up making a movie,” Nora says.

Charlotte says, “Oh, I shot one with Shaun.”

Lexi says, “I shot one with Bonny.”

I say, “I’ll show you guys mine later.”

~~~

Ray’s in the hall when we go out. “I was just about to knock,” he says.

They’re not even twins anymore. Something behind the eyes, some core difference I can see as easily as I can their skin, their hair. Like identical necklaces except one’s silver and the other gold.

The girls flank me and, for once, I want them there.

“I wanted to apologize,” he says. “For all of it. But I also wanted to say . . .” He looks at my friends. “Actually can we talk in private for a second?”

I say, “No, we can’t.”

I don’t believe that Ray actually hypnotized Bill. I don’t believe that one day, something as simple as a song could cause a man to lose his mind. I choose to believe that Ray will get help, move on, and that sanity will prevail. That doesn’t mean I want to be alone with him.

“Fine, then I just wanted to say that that first night was really fun and special. I liked you. I still do. I can’t think of the last time I felt like I clicked that way with someone. I’m sorry I messed it up. I’m sorry I messed everything up.”

“Why did you even get me involved?” I ask.

“I don’t know. I had this feeling that you could, like, use a diversion. I thought maybe in the end you’d think it was all sort of fun. When you said you liked Hitchcock, it was just all too perfect. For a second I imagined us as these partners in crime. When I realized
~~~

I shouldn't get you involved it was too late, I'd already gotten you involved."

I nod and think back to that first night. How dazzling he'd seemed. How charming. How new. But I don't see movie-star dashing anymore. I don't see a future. I only see what he's not. His negative. His opposite.

He hasn't actually messed up everything, though.

At least, not for me.

I'm the writer/director of my life.

~~~

```
EXT -- HIGH SCHOOL -- DAY

A group of girls are gathered on the front
steps. Talking, laughing. A group of guys are
drawn to them, walk over. One of the girls,
NATALIE, is the first to see them. She moves
out of the group and steps up to one of the
guys. He's smiling in a predatory sort of way.

              NATALIE
        You don't even remember me, do
        you?

The guys all laugh, uncomfortable.

              NATALIE
        You sexually assaulted me at a
        party.
```
~~~

~~~

Michael wanted to walk off the ship together, so he's waiting for us all by the midship disembarkation point. A couple is struggling with their children, one of whom is crying, "But I don't want to go home." People are smiling at them sympathetically; not Lexi, though. Lexi looks tired—and ready to go home. She'll probably go right back to life with Jason, and it's none of my business, really.

What happens on a cruise stays on a cruise.

Charlotte looks sort of sad; like this was a place where she could just *be*. She'll take the braids out and go back to straightening and ponytails, and people in school will keep looking at her like she's two different people instead of the one she really is.

"I have one more question," I say to Michael, taking a final look around the Atrium with its glass elevators and balconies and that massive crystal anchor that never got the best of us. I watch the people who are lined up nicely to leave and feel a weird sort of camaraderie with them. We all chose this crazy thing to do together, and we all survived it. No one jumped, turns out. No one with some horrible plague skipped out on the antibacterial wipes and spread misery. Maybe it's true that we're all the worst kind of tourists, but I feel a certain kind of awe anyway.

"What's the question?"

"At the B and B, the doctor said something weird. He said he never intended to hurt anyone, which was more than Ray could say. What did he mean?"

"I *really* don't want to tell you that."
~~~

"All the more reason for me to know."

"I'm sorry, folks," a cruise person says. "We need to keep moving."

Then I'm with my group and he's in another line and he says, "I'll text you or call or something."

And we're like the lead couple in some old movie involving train platforms—steam and whistles and hats and newspapers—and the crowd carries us away from each other and we're powerless to do anything about it.

Star-crossed.

Doomed.

Roll credits.

~~~

I want to kiss the ground, but of course don't.

The bus is a greenhouse. My mother wilts against my father's shoulder in the seats in front of me, and I think about my room, my tiny dangling dancer above my bed with a ribbon swirl above her head.

I think about what it'll feel like to walk into school on Monday, carrying what feels like a secret.

I close my eyes and lean my head against the window and look forward to the end of the bus ride and the end of the whole journey home, the end of all this motion. I plan on standing still for a good long while.

I consider what I'm going to say to Nora's brother the next time I see him—about that night, about the friends he keeps.

"Why didn't you tell me?" I ask Lexi beside me, opening my eyes. "About Nora and Paul?"
~~~

"I only figured it out after he died," she says. "I guess I thought it might be best swept under the carpet."

"You were wrong." I elbow her.

"Maybe," she says. "Maybe not. I mean, what would it have changed?"

"It's not about that," I say. "It's about it being, you know, the truth."

My phone buzzes texts from Michael at me.

I don't even want to read them.

The cruise was a spell that life cast over me, and it's broken.

I wonder if there are movies I haven't seen that have falling-*out*-of-love montages.

~~~

Mr. Cassidy had been right about *The Poseidon Adventure*. I went back to it. It was an itch I had to scratch. I needed to know how many of them, if any, survived, and how. Because it couldn't just be that everyone died at the end. There had to be more to it—and to life—than that.

I watched alone on my phone in bed one night, the lights out, blankets pulled up tight, and I cried when the handful of survivors reached the hull of the ship and heard a tapping sound. A rescue team was cutting through metal to pull them out to safety. I closed my eyes and wondered what it would feel like—to see, for the first time in days, the brilliant white light of the sun.

~~~

Ray's on a travel soccer team.

Hypnotized some guys in the locker room as a joke.

Thought one guy on the other team was a jerk; he was like bragging about cheating on his girlfriend or something.

Ray told him the world would be a better place without him and that he should just go kill himself.

The guy died like the next day.

Ray saw it in the paper or something.

I see it for what it is. A crazy coincidence.

But Ray was a mess.

I don't know how the doctor would know that except he still has family in town and there were some rumors.

But hypnosis isn't real.

You know that, right?

Right?

~~~

I drop my phone. The smack is decisive. I don't have to pick it up to know the glass has shattered. I picture water pouring out from that human aquarium, flooding everything around.

It's for the best.

I'll get a new one.

I'll have a new number.

I'll pretend none of it ever happened. I'll pretend it was all a dream. Something I must have imagined—a movie I wrote and can rewrite.

If I tell myself that enough times, I will start to believe it.

"I'll say one thing about those twins," Lexi says. "They sure snapped you out of whatever you were in."

I'm starting a new draft right now—a page-one rewrite.

"Natalie?" Lexi asks. "You okay?"
~~~

I close my eyes again—"Never been better"—and let the unrelenting sun warm my eyelids and then the rest of me, too.

This is Natalie.

~~~

INT. BUS -- DAY

Two identical twin teenage boys, MICHAEL and RAY, are sitting next to each other. Michael, on the right, has just put his phone down.

RAY
I think I could have fallen in love with her.

MICHAEL
I think I did.

~~~

INT. BASEMENT -- DAY

A teenage boy, PAUL, and girl, NORA, are making out on a plaid couch.

NORA
We really shouldn't.

PAUL
She never has to know.

~~~

EXT. CRUISE SHIP DECK -- NIGHT

Two teenage girls, LEXI and NORA, stand beside each other. Light wind. Clear skies.

LEXI

Where do you think you heard about that hypnosis thing anyway?

NORA

It was something Paul said after a soccer game, but I didn't think anything of it at the time.

The ship coughs gray exhaust from its chimney into the night sky. They both look up as the smoke briefly obscures the stars, then, just as quickly, disappears.

FADE OUT
~~~

• ACKNOWLEDGMENTS •

David Dunton at Harvey Klinger Agency has been helping to direct the cruise of my career for a good long while now. Getting Sarah Shumway at Bloomsbury to come on board with us was a smart move for sure. Both of you have earned stateroom upgrades a hundred times over.

Thanks to the rest of the incredible Bloomsbury team for making this whole endeavor feel like smooth sailing: Erica Barmash, Anna Bernard, Bethany Buck, Alexis Castellanos, Nicholas Church, Beth Eller, Alona Fryman, Emily Gerbner, Cristina Gilbert, Courtney Griffin, Melissa Kavonic, Cindy Loh, Lizzy Mason, Shae McDaniel, Patricia McHugh, Brittany Mitchell, Oona Patrick, Emily Ritter, Claire Stetzer, and Ellen Whitaker.

Thanks again to the design team of Donna Mark, Amanda Bartlett, and Kimi Weart.

Special shout out to Jennifer Lynn Barnes.

Huge thanks to Nick, Ellie, and Violet for being such attentive research assistants.

And a hat tip to the late great Great-Aunt Helen for taking me on my first cruise many moons ago.